**"Oh, what am I going to do with him?"
Ann murmured.**

"You mean me, I hope?" a husky voice asked.

She spun around, shocked to find she wasn't alone in the staff room. "Jeff, how did you get in here? This room is off-limits to guests."

"Piece of cake, Annie," he said, taking her into his arms and kissing her long and hard before she could refuse him.

She melted against him, softly moaning in surrender.

"Run away with me, love," he whispered. "I'll worship at your feet . . . not to mention the rest of your gorgeous body." He waggled his brows like Groucho Marx.

In a fog of confusion and desire, Ann simply stared at him.

"Admit it," he said. "I turn you on."

She smiled winsomely at his choice of words. "You sure do." Then her smile became sensual. "But I'll bet ev̶̶ ̶ ̶̶ ̶ ̶ ̶̶ got that I do the s̶ ̶ ̶

"I wo̶ ̶ ̶ ̶ ̶ ̶ ̶ ̶ ̶ ̶ust what I've bee̶ ̶ ̶ ̶ ̶ ̶ ̶ ̶ ̶cked his hands a̶ ̶ ̶ ̶ ̶ ̶ ̶r closer. "I want e̶ ̶ ̶ ̶ ̶ ̶ give . . ."

WHAT ARE *LOVESWEPT* ROMANCES?

They are stories of true romance and touching emotion. We believe those two very important ingredients are constants in our highly sensual and very believable stories in the *LOVESWEPT* line. Our goal is to give you, the reader, stories of consistently high quality that may sometimes make you laugh, sometimes make you cry, but are always fresh and creative and contain many delightful surprises within their pages.

Most romance fans read an enormous number of books. Those they truly love, they keep. Others may be traded with friends and soon forgotten. We hope that each *LOVESWEPT* romance will be a treasure—a "keeper." We will always try to publish

LOVE STORIES YOU'LL NEVER FORGET
BY AUTHORS YOU'LL ALWAYS REMEMBER

The Editors

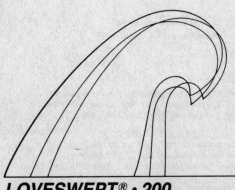

LOVESWEPT® • 200

Joan Bramsch
With No Reservations

BANTAM BOOKS
TORONTO • NEW YORK • LONDON • SYDNEY • AUCKLAND

To my daughter, Mary

Crystal prisms of sadness, gladness,
Flow in sparkling, shimmering streams,
Revealing the rainbow spectrum of her nurturing
  heart.

I love you.

WITH NO RESERVATIONS
A Bantam Book / July 1987

If you would be interested in receiving protective vinyl
covers for your Loveswept books, please write to this address
for information:

Loveswept
Bantam Books
P.O. Box 985
Hicksville, NY 11802

ISBN 0-553-21808-5

Published simultaneously in the United States and Canada

PRINTED IN THE UNITED STATES OF AMERICA

O   0 9 8 7 6 5 4 3 2 1

One

"Can you take care of me, please? I'd like to check in."

Ann Waverly looked up from her work at the registration desk and stared at the man through her large tortoise-shell-framed glasses. Good heavens, she thought. *Someone* should take care of him!

The man was bedraggled, unshaven, and almost asleep on his feet. What terrible hardship had he endured? His sandy hair was tousled, his clothes rumpled and torn. Most astounding of all, how had he gotten here, to the middle of urban America? It wasn't every day that a man in his condition strode into the River Regency, the most exclusive hotel in St. Charles, Missouri.

All these thoughts tumbled through Ann's mind in a matter of seconds. She schooled her features— sedate, tranquil—then smiled and asked the first question any reservation clerk worth her salt should ask.

"Do you have a reservation, sir?"

The man leaned heavily against the counter; his glazed blue eyes stared across the lobby. "The name's Jeffrey Madison. The reservation was confirmed yesterday."

Ann rapidly punched his name into the computer. Gazing at the screen, she was dismayed by what she saw printed there. "I'm very sorry, Mr. Madison, but your room was released when you didn't arrive before eight o'clock this evening."

And she was sorry. Jeffrey Madison appeared to be dead on his feet. Then he turned to her, and his gaze seemed to chill and boil at the same time. She forgot her compassion because the hair on the back of her neck suddenly stood at attention. Unable to break away from his furious glare, she was glad that a high marble counter separated her body from his.

Jeffrey Madison studied the woman who was keeping him from his bed. Her dark hair was pulled back into a neat, smooth bun and her blue eyes were shielded by expensive-looking glasses. She used a minimum of makeup, and her navy blue uniform was adorned only by her name tag. *Ann Waverly*, it said. He intended to remember that name. Forever!

"What the hell do you mean, Ms. Waverly?" he asked. Pushed beyond his endurance, he raised his voice and gestured broadly. "A room was reserved. Yesterday. I need sleep. Tonight. Just find me another room in this damn place so I can get some rest."

His performance did nothing to reassure Ann. She didn't think the hotel needed to cater to a madman. Not on her shift anyway. "Perhaps the Lasta Motel down the highway has a vacancy, sir. I'll be glad to make the call."

"Are you kidding?" he exploded. *"The Lasta Motel?"*

He looked at her as if she'd just dropped in from Mars, Ann thought, when in reality it was *his* bloodshot eyes that were beginning to radiate an otherworldly glow. Any second now he'd send a zap across the counter that would melt the silver in her back teeth. Imagining she could already feel that menacing heat, she took one small step backward . . . for her own good health.

"Look, lady, I had a reservation. I'm staying here tonight." He jerked his thumb over his shoulder. "Even if I have to sleep in the damn potted palms."

Ann kept smiling, although she felt like sticking out her tongue at him. She told herself she had to get the man to leave before he attracted a crowd. It was ten-thirty and quite a few guests were still in the garden lounge in the center of the huge lobby. Just as she was about to speak, Mr. Gillian, the night manager, appeared at her side.

"What seems to be the problem here, *Miss* Waverly?"

Oh, he *would* have to come out now, she fumed to herself, grimly accepting his condescending tone. He pronounced the word "Miss" as if it were a sin to be single. Before she could explain, he brusquely excused her, then aimed an effusive smile at the disheveled man on the other side of the counter.

"Perhaps I can help you, sir," Mr. Gillian said.

"Please overlook the night clerk's lack of understanding. She's a trainee."

Ann stalked to the back office. She glanced at her watch and realized her shift was over. Checking to make sure she still had her room key in her jacket pocket, she trudged to the elevator. It was glass on three sides, and as it lifted her to the second floor, she could see the registration desk. She sighed when she saw the night manager give the seedy Mr. Madison a key and another simpering smile.

"That little fiasco was not an auspicious beginning, Annie," she muttered.

When Jeffrey took the key, he experienced a pang of conscience. "Look," he said. "I don't want Ms. Waverly to get into trouble. This wasn't her fault. She was undoubtedly following house rules."

Mr. Gillian stopped smiling, but assured Jeffrey that *Miss* Waverly had nothing to fear. "After all, Mr. Madison, she's *only* a trainee. Thank you for being so charitable."

Jeffrey grunted unintelligibly, then wearily found his way to his room. He paused in the bathroom for a long, cool drink of water. When he realized he was still holding his battered knapsack, he tossed it into the corner of the bedroom.

Yawning and groaning on the same breath, he dropped his jacket inside the closet, bent to untie his hiking boots, then staggered toward the welcoming oasis of his clean bed, dropping clothes and boots along the way. He sank onto the foot of the bed, pulled off one remaining sock, and collapsed across the mattress. Slowly he turned and crawled under the covers like a bear about to hibernate.

His last thought as he drifted into unconsciousness was that the manager had acted like a grade-A jerk, and that he would check the next day to make sure the attractive *Ms.* Waverly had not been hassled.

In her own room, Ann was getting ready for bed. For the hundredth time she thought she probably should have her head examined. What had she been thinking when she'd accepted the unorthodox challenge from Vanessa Cummings, owner of the River Regency?

"I must have been out of my mind," she mumbled, brushing her teeth with unrelenting vigor.

She lifted her head and peered at her reflection in the mirror. Large blue eyes, the irises outlined with indigo, stared back. Her small, straight nose was shiny. When she looked at her mouth and saw the foaming toothpaste bubbling from her pursed lips, she burst out laughing.

"See?" she said, leaning over to finish her chore. "You've gone mad!"

She pulled the pins from her hair, and the sable locks fell to her waist. As she brushed her hair, she reassessed the reasons that she'd decided to come to St. Charles in the first place.

For the last seven years she had worked for a Chicago hotel, part of an international chain. And though she'd risen from clerk to public relations associate during those years, she had known it was time to find a position with more authority. Personal assistant to the owner of a four-star hotel had seemed like the right move.

She couldn't deny the attraction of the new job, but there had been a catch to the offer. Before she could begin her formal duties, she would have to sample all the diversified jobs executed by the general staff on a revolving daily schedule. It would take a month.

Vanessa Cummings believed her strange request was logical. "If you know the jobs, you'll be in a better position to handle complaints," she had told Ann.

But Ann quite frankly believed Vanessa Cummings wanted to test her mettle, though her new boss had sweetened the pot by providing this lovely room until Ann could find an apartment near the hotel. She also thought the job was an opportunity she couldn't afford to pass by, no matter how kooky this idea seemed. Anyway, it was right up Ann's alley. She liked to gamble, so long as it involved risking only her own skin.

She turned out the light and crawled into bed, then released a long sigh and relaxed. As she drifted to sleep, she wondered where Mr. Gillian had put the wild man. She pictured the unlikely guest in her mind. He was tall, and although he was obviously exhausted, he looked as if he might wrestle bears or bulls, or even mountain lions, for a living. Shuddering, she decided she was glad she'd been dismissed. Another minute under that sizzling stare and she would have gotten a free perm.

•   •   •

By ten o'clock the following morning Ann had been working almost two hours. Today she was a house-keeper, and she'd been given a list of the cleaning chores required for each of her assigned rooms.

She pushed her cleaning cart along the well-lighted gold-carpeted hallway, which on one side looked out over the lobby. The central part of the hotel was open, rising twelve stories to a glass roof. Ann paused to lean far over the sturdy oak rail and look down at the garden lounge, the bubbling fountain, the ebony grand piano, the intimate seating areas. Straightening slowly, she tipped her head back to gaze up at the fluffy clouds racing like celestial char-iots across the blue sky. It was true, she thought, not for the first time: The River Regency's architec-ture was spectacular.

She continued on to Room 604. She smoothed her hair and the skirt of her rose-colored uniform, and knocked once. There was no response, and she knocked again, harder. When no one answered, she unlocked the door with her master key and entered the room. Quickly she assessed the bathroom. One glass had been used and she replaced it, but noth-ing else had been disturbed.

When she walked out of the bathroom, she stum-bled. Glancing down, she saw a boot lying on its side. A trail of clothing led into the darkened bed-room. Like Gretel, she followed, picking up the boot, a sock, a second scuffed boot, a gamey pair of faded jeans which could have stood by themselves, a soft blue-plaid shirt that smelled like woodsmoke, and, finally, a pair of navy briefs.

Just when she realized she was short one sock, a sunbeam peeked through the drapes and spotlighted the elusive gray wool sock at the foot of the bed. Muttering to herself about sloppy guests, she leaned over to pick it up—and came nose to toes with a large bare foot!

Someone was here . . . in the bed, she realized. Was he dead? Frozen in her crouched position, she continued to stare at the foot until the man groaned, kicked off his covers, and turned over. He began snoring, loud enough, it seemed, to rattle the windows.

Reassured that the guest was very much alive, Ann retreated slowly, stealthily. She kept her gaze glued to a crescent-shaped scar on the bottom of the man's heel, but her peripheral vision nevertheless noticed the rest of him—nude—and lying now on his stomach.

She paused for just a moment and let her inquisitive gaze meander across the tantalizing expanse of his relaxed muscular body. Suddenly, she caught her breath. Of all the people to stumble upon! she thought. That glorious specimen of the male species was the man who'd checked in last night.

Taking another step backward, she berated herself for looking. But her self was having none of it. It was a safe bet no one would ever know, and so, feeling assured, she chanced a last lingering look.

If there was anything in this world she truly appreciated, it was the bold, lean lines of the male form. For Ann, a well-developed body was a joy to behold. She considered it living sculpture. And if she didn't get out of this room quickly, she was going to get into trouble because she was sorely tempted to examine this intriguing three-dimensional work of art with more than her eyes!

Sighing wistfully, she replaced each item of clothing exactly where she'd found it, then sneaked out the door, taking the Do Not Disturb sign with her.

Whistling softly, she leaned against the wall and began to breathe again. She had to admit, Jeffrey Madison—in nature's garb, so to speak—was certainly a surprise. Yes, he'd appeared to be very strong and well-built when she met him the night before. But she would never have guessed that beneath those tattered mountainman clothes lay such a fabulous body. Hercules? A Superman? A Rocky?

"Definitely, a Rocky," she murmured as she moved to the next room. "And surely a ten!" She whistled again, then knocked so hard on the door of the room that she hurt her knuckles and alarmed the occupants.

The hours passed quickly. Ann had plenty to keep her busy. But at odd moments—when she was smoothing the covers on a bed or running the vacuum—her mind supplied a most graphic image of Jeffrey Madison sprawled nude upon his rumpled sheets. Inconsequentially she wondered how he'd gotten that crescent scar. Maybe he'd been kicking at one of those mountain lions he wrestled and got swiped by a claw, she thought, picturing the battle in her vivid imagination. And of course Mr. Madison had won. There was no doubt in her mind.

• • •

Jeffrey's mother, owner of the River Regency, wakened him in midafternoon when she phoned.

"Oh, darling," she said when she heard his groggy voice. "I'm sorry I disturbed you. You should have slept at Mountainview before you flew all the way from Utah."

"Hey, Legs, you call, I haul," he said lightly.

"Did you find the lost little boy?" she asked.

"Yup, all safe and sound."

"I'm so relieved, son."

"Me too. He must have been scared to death, but he didn't show it." He yawned and stretched. "Are you still losing convention business?"

"Yes, two more last week. Since you're the investigator, I hope you can catch the guilty party soon, though, Lord knows, I've asked you often enough to take over here."

"Now, don't start that again, Mom."

Jeffrey had been raised in the hotel business. His parents had owned the Mountainview Inn for three decades until four years ago, when his father had died suddenly. His mother had sold out, taken one year to travel, two more to get herself pulled back together, then had purchased the River Regency.

The only time he'd been here was before she'd taken over and brought in new management. Since then he'd stayed away on purpose because he was sure she needed some space to prove to herself she could manage alone. Personally, Jeffrey never doubted his mother's abilities. He believed she could handle anything in the hotel business. He also knew she loved it. He, on the other hand, did not.

Jeffrey had chosen to use his knowledge of the business world to investigate white-collar crime. Embezzling, patent fraud, the theft and sale of corporate secrets were a few of his specialties. He loved his work because he was a risk taker, had been since he was a child. And he knew how to keep a secret.

"When did you get in?" his mother asked.

"About ten-thirty last night. And it was *some experience*!" He purposely exaggerated the circumstances. "The first person I met was a woman named Ann Waverly. Boy, have you got her brainwashed. She just kept smiling and telling me my reservation had been released. Finally I was given this dinky little room."

"There are no dinky little rooms at the River Regency, young man."

He chuckled at her imperious tone. "Well, I feel closed in."

"You'll get your suite. Within twenty-four hours. Those are house rules."

"You run a tight ship, ma'am."

"But it's sprung a leak somewhere, so let's get busy." Vanessa was sure one of her employees was tipping off another hotel about convention inquiries, and they'd been undercutting Regency's bids.

"Do you have any suspects?" Jeffrey asked.

"Three." She named the public relations director, the convention coordinator, and the general manager. "They're all new, you know. The only person I brought from Utah is Charles."

"It'll be good to see him."

Charles Jones had been only eighteen years old when he was hired to be Sam and Vanessa Cummings's chauffeur. The following year Jeffrey had been born, and it seemed natural when the two formed a strong bond, almost like younger and older brother. Charles had helped Jeffrey's parents curb their son's youthful headstrong impetuosity. After Jeffrey reached adulthood, he admitted that it had probably taken all three of them to guide him through the maze of adolescence.

"Remember," his mother said now, "you don't know either Charles or me."

"Right. Are you in the penthouse now, Mom? I thought you'd come down to greet your only son."

"I'm in the hospital."

Jeffrey's teasing vanished instantly. He listened intently as Vanessa explained that she'd worried herself into a gall bladder attack, but was feeling much better now. The doctor had insisted that she have a complete physical checkup, so she would stay in the hospital for the rest of the week.

"I've been telling you to take it a little easier, Mom. I wish you would."

"And I will, son . . . as soon as you give me my grandbabies."

Jeffrey ran his hand through his sleep-tousled hair. "Now, Mama, you know I'm kinda old-fashioned about that. I have to find a wife first."

"Well?"

"You're too sexy to be a grandma."

"Like hell I am! I've said it before and I'll say it again— "

"I know, Mom."

Together they recited, "Thirty-four years is a damn long time to wait for another baby!"

"Well, it is!"

"I'm working on it."

"Are you even looking, young man?"

"Sure, I am. All the time," he said with a lilt in his voice. Unheralded, the image of the attractive Ann Waverly came into his mind. "I love you, Mom. See you later."

"You will not see me. I don't want this caper queered."

Jeffrey chuckled as he hung up the phone, then he rolled out of bed. On his way to the bathroom he picked up his clothes and boots and dumped them in the closet. In the bathroom he reached for his glass, but had to unwrap a clean one.

Funny, he thought. He could have sworn he'd drunk about a gallon of water last night. Shrugging, he turned on the shower, then stepped beneath the hard spray and scrubbed off two days worth of grime. As he dried himself, he idly surveyed his reflection in the hazy mirror. His sandy hair was sun-streaked and thick. One woman had told him his wide-set eyes were bluer than a rain-washed Utah sky. His face and neck were perpetually tanned, and his muscular body revealed his love of outdoor activities in any weather, any season.

When he pulled a clean knit shirt from his knapsack, he winced as the fabric irritated a cut on his hand. "Damn," he muttered, sucking on his knuckle. He wished he'd worn heavier gloves. The rocks had cut his hands badly. He tugged on the shirt and a fresh pair of jeans, then called his Mountainview office.

"Hi, Kim," he said when his assistant answered the phone. "Anything going on?"

"There's always something going on, boss. You know that."

"Can you handle it?"

"Sure."

"Then I won't worry about it," he replied. "I'll be setting the trap for my mom's informer in the next few days. I'll give each of the targets identical details about a phony upcoming national convention. The only difference is that I'll give each of them a different company name. When the bids arrive—I'll use the office address—the one we receive from Mom's competitor will be linked to the guilty party."

"Neat idea, boss," said Kim. "Ingenious."

"Yeah, well, what can I say," he answered, chuckling happily. "Will you ask Les to pack enough clothes for me for two weeks and send them ASAP? It looks like I'm going to be here for a while."

"Your bags are already packed, Jeff. We'll air-freight them to you."

"What a team!"

"We aim to please."

"Thanks, Kim. I'll keep in touch."

After Jeffrey had hung up, his stomach gave a mighty growl. He massaged his middle, wondering when he'd last eaten. Yesterday. Afternoon? No wonder he was hungry. He needed food—fast. He slipped his room key and wallet into separate pockets and strode to the door. When he opened it he noticed the Do Not Disturb sign on the outside. He couldn't remember placing it there. "Man, I must have been walking in my sleep last night," he mumbled.

Later that evening, when Jeffrey strolled into the lobby, Mr. Gillian caught his attention. "Good evening, Mr. Madison. Your suite is ready for occupancy, sir. Suite 1108."

Not bad, Jeffrey thought as he exchanged keys with the man. Then he remembered the trainee. "Oh, by the way, I hope you didn't discipline Ms. Waverly." He glanced around. "I haven't seen her today."

"Miss Waverly is still with us." Mr. Gillian's tone revealed he was less than pleased.

"Very good, Mr. Gillian." The look in Jeffrey's eyes let the man know there would have been hell to pay if she'd been fired. "I'd like a wake-up call for seven."

By nine o'clock Wednesday morning Jeffrey had swum fifty laps in the hotel pool, showered, shaved, dressed, and consumed a large breakfast. He was determined not to waste another day. He wasn't used to inactivity. In fact, he hated it.

He belonged in the mountains, he thought as he left the hotel restaurant, heading for the elevators. All thoughts of the great outdoors fled, though, when he spotted Ann Waverly seated behind an ornate desk in the lobby. The small gold-lettered sign on the mahogany surface said: CONCIERGE. She was talking animatedly to a woman, obviously doing her best to please a guest. Jeffrey slipped behind a potted palm to watch her unobserved.

Damn, he thought, she had on those huge goggles again. How was a man supposed to see what she was thinking? Her hair was pulled back into the same smooth, businesslike bun, and she was wearing the unappealing uniform she'd worn two nights ago. She did, however, fill out that uniform very well, as far as he could see.

But it was her smile that really attracted his gaze. It wasn't a phony smile. On the contrary, it was genuine, expressing her pleasure in her work. He wondered, could a man measure the goodness of a woman by her smile? It was worth investigating, he decided. When the guest got up to leave, he strolled from his hiding place.

Ann noticed the tall man walking toward her. He looked familiar, but she couldn't quite place him. Suddenly she recognized him. It was Jeffrey Madison, clean-shaven and wearing a sport jacket over a cotton shirt and dress trousers. My, he was handsome, she thought, smiling shyly. She was glad to see him, but was embarrassed over their last two meetings—one of which he didn't even know about! —and wished he hadn't seen her.

"Hi, Ms. Waverly," he greeted her. "Coming up in the world?"

"You might say that."

Her lips curved into an impish grin as she realized she would have recognized Jeffrey in a second had she been able to get a peek at his left heel. Her grin didn't quite register with him. He obviously had his mind on something else, for his blond brows drew together in a thoughtful scowl.

"Won't that manager take you back?" he asked. "I'll speak to him at once."

"That really isn't necessary, Mr. Madison."

"Certainly it is." He looked over at the registration desk, hoping to see Mr. Gillian.

"But . . . but . . ."

Jeffrey swung his gaze back to Ann, trying to see past the reflection in her glasses. Was she afraid to make trouble? he wondered. Then another thought came to mind.

"Are you covering for someone?" he asked, grinning. "Without permission?"

Sighing, she straightened a stack of tourist brochures, then removed her glasses. She looked up, her dark-lashed eyes boldly meeting his inquisitive gaze. "I might as well tell you. You aren't going to stop till I do. I'm in a new-concept training program, doing a different job every day."

"For what reason?" he asked absently as he stared into her eyes. Ann Waverly, he thought, had the most beautiful, expressive eyes he'd ever seen. Their indigo-blue color was unusual, and a definite threat to his nervous system. Suddenly he felt the need to sit down, and did so instantly.

"It's designed to see if I'm worthy of the Regency," she said in answer to his question.

Jeffrey thought her explanation exemplary. He wished all his mother's employees shared Ann's attitude. "What will you do the rest of this week?" he asked.

"Tomorrow I work in the kitchen, and on Friday I'm in the luggage storeroom."

He snorted with disgust. "Luggage? That's no work for a woman."

Ann glared directly into his clear blue eyes. "I will be working one of the jobs, Mr. Madison. I'd like to point out to you that women work everywhere in this hotel. We're an equal opportunity establishment."

"Yeah, any one of you can get a hernia," he said, silently vowing to discuss this edict with his mother.

"Mr. Madison," Ann sputtered, her eyes blazing, "you are a dyed-in-the-wool chauvinist bully."

Jeffrey's scowl disappeared instantly. Grinning again, he reached for her hand and smoothed his roughened thumb over her knuckles. "Uh-uh," he said, shaking his head. "I just don't want you to hurt your hands, Ann. Yours are made for gentler work. For pleasure." His voice was a whisper as he lifted her hand to his lips and kissed her fingertips.

His gallant gesture prompted a sigh to slip from Ann's lips, and she simply could not force herself to withdraw from his touch.

"Aren't you about ready to take a break?" he murmured, continuing to hold her hand. His smoky gaze captured hers. "Let's have a cup of coffee."

"I'm very sorry, sir." And she was. "Employees aren't allowed to fraternize with the guests." She smiled to soften her refusal and retrieved her hand.

Jeffrey was so smitten with her enchanting smile, he almost admitted he wasn't a paying guest. Catching himself just in time, he tried to cajole her into accepting his invitation anyway.

"What harm can come from a cup of coffee and a little innocent conversation? Come on, just one cup?"

Ann had to steel herself against his gentle persuasion. His firm lips curved into a whimsical smile, and his blue eyes were warm. "It's a house rule, Mr. Madison. And a good one, I believe."

Ann's reckless spirit and more sensible self warred within her. She was able to admit she'd like to get to know Jeffrey Madison better. But she also knew her interest in this man could get her into a whole lot of trouble.

Jeffrey was watching her eyes, sensing her indecision, and he believed he could change her mind. The challenge was very nearly overwhelming. "Ann, won't you reconsider?" he asked in his most seductive voice as he gently stroked her hand again.

Smiling a bittersweet smile, she slipped her hand away from his, realizing how close she was to accepting his invitation. "Thank you, Mr. Madison, but I really can't accept. I hope you'll understand."

Jeffrey was surprised by his tenacity. He told himself he was being so persistent because he might obtain some useful information about the convention tipster from her, but deep down he knew that was a flimsy excuse. He was simply incredibly attracted to Ann Waverly, elusive woman that she was.

Ann studied Jeffrey, hoping he would stay, yet conversely wishing he'd disappear. He was too tempting. She could still feel the warmth of his kiss on her fingertips. This was not the time to become involved with a dangerously handsome man. Furthermore, he was a guest of the hotel. Period! End of discussion. She needed every bit of her energy to meet the challenge she'd accepted from her boss.

"So you're concierge for the day?" he asked.

She nodded.

His tanned features relaxed; his grin warmed her fluttering heart. "I come from a little town in Utah. Mountainview."

"I know."

"You do?" He was startled, then he chuckled. "Ah, yes, the registration card. Handy things to have around."

"I guess."

"I'm delighted that you were interested enough to look."

She lowered her gaze and her cheeks glowed with color. "I think the word to describe my feelings would be 'curious.' "

"Or 'terrified'?" he suggested, tipping her chin up with his finger and smiling. "I know I bellowed like a wounded moose the other night."

"Well, not terrified," she said. "More like alarmed." She laughed softly. "You looked like you'd been stranded on one of your mountains for months."

"Only two days," he said. "But they were long ones. I led a volunteer wilderness rescue team at Mountainview. When you and I first met, I'd just returned from a two-day search for a little boy."

"Did you find him?" she asked, almost afraid to

know the answer. Jeffrey had looked so exhausted that night. He may not have been successful.

"We found him, safe and sound," he said. "But we were lucky. He knew enough to find shelter and stay put."

"I'm so glad to hear it. And it explains why you looked the way you did that night." Her eyes sparkled with sudden tears of relief. "I think only a very special person would risk his life in order to save another's."

Jeffrey was uncomfortable with her sincere praise. Her glistening gaze, her warm smile, were genuine expressions of her feelings. Of that he was sure. "That's nice of you to say, Ann, but it was a team effort." He shook his head and chuckled. "You should have seen that little guy leap into his dad's arms and try to hug his mom at the same time with the little strength he had left." He gazed into Ann's eyes. "I thought he'd never let go of them. Or they let go of him."

"I don't suppose a search always ends so happily."

The grin slid from his lips. "No, and those are the times I die a little myself. It's hard. Real hard."

Ann tentatively reached out a hand and covered his clenched fist. "I'm sorry I brought it up, Mr. Madison. Forgive me?"

The smile returned to his eyes first, then his mouth curved into a mischievous grin. "Only if you call me by my first name."

"I couldn't. The house rules."

"Sure you can. Look at me and watch my lips."

Oh, that was very easy to do, she decided, lifting her gaze.

"Now, repeat after me. Jeffrey." He cocked his head and waited.

"Jeffrey," she murmured.

"Ah, Ann, that sounded wonderful. Say it again."

"Jeffrey," she repeated, then realized what she was doing. This would never do. "I have a question, Jeffrey," she said, trying to change the subject to more neutral ground. "What was the big hurry to get here? You should have rested first."

"I had an important meeting scheduled," he answered, careful to be vague. "Anyway, I don't often get to the big city. Let's see you do your stuff."

For the next half hour Ann gave him chapter and verse about the sights, sounds, and educational tours in the St. Charles area. Jeffrey listened patiently, asking questions, making choices.

"Excellent work, Ms. Waverly," he said finally. "I'll be sure to tell management how helpful you've been."

"I'm only doing my job, sir," she replied, but couldn't keep from smiling at his compliment.

"Will you make reservations for the two tours I've indicated?" he asked. "I'd like to have confirmation now."

It took her another fifteen minutes to make the calls. When she was through, she sighed with relief and smiled at Jeffrey. "Everything is confirmed, Mr. Madison. I hope you enjoy your tours."

Jeffrey tipped his head to one side, rubbing the back of his neck as if he were ill at ease. "Ah . . .

would you mind making those reservations for two? I'd like to invite a lady."

Ann wasn't quite able to mask her features when she gritted her teeth, but after one unguarded moment she smiled again. "Certainly, sir. Your guest's name?"

"Ann Waverly."

She moaned, frustrated. "But I've told you, I can't go out with you."

"You'd be my tour guide."

"I would not!" she shot back, and was incredulous when he grinned engagingly. That grin tunneled straight into her heart.

"Others would think so," he said.

"Perhaps, but I'd know different."

"So would I," he said softly, stroking her hand slowly. It was a vivid reminder of the touch of his warm lips. He glanced down when he felt a trembling beneath his fingers. "I'd like to kiss you, Ann," he murmured. "Come away with me, away from this hotel and your job. Travel with me to the land where wishes come true." He gave her hand a gentle squeeze. "And, Annie, I *do* wish to kiss you . . . again and again."

Her lips parted and her breath caught, and Jeffrey pressed his advantage. "Speak with your heart, Annie," he whispered, leaning closer. "Let's live dangerously. We can fool the world for a few hours."

Oh, no! she thought in dismay. She longed to say yes, to give in to the temptation to spend an entire day with him, gazing into his eyes, listening to his deep voice. . . . And that kind of challenge was just her cup of tea. But she couldn't, she told herself. She absolutely, positively could not.

"It wouldn't be ethical," she said. "I'm truly sorry."

He frowned, not accustomed to negative responses in any area of his life. "But I want to spend some time with you. Alone." He laughed gruffly. "What's it take to get a date with you? A move out of the hotel?"

Her musical laughter and dancing blue eyes were almost his undoing. "Surely, a date with me can't mean that much. You'll be gone soon. I'd feel guilty if you took such drastic action."

"I may be here for some time," he argued doggedly. "It's indefinite."

"Oh? What business are you in?"

Secrets, secrets! complained his churning brain. Tell the truth, but make it evasive. "I'm . . . ah . . . a headhunter."

"In what field?"

"Corporate executives." Well done, he congratulated himself.

"That must be an interesting profession. Traveling around the country, interviewing all types of people."

He shook his head, searching for a way to get her off the track. "It's boring as hell, Ann." He favored her with another dazzling smile, enjoying the pink flush on her cheeks. "I'd rather talk about our trip."

"I've told you, Mr. Madison—"

"Jeffrey . . . please," he said coaxingly.

"All right. Jeffrey. But the answer is still no." She tried hard to keep her voice firm and unwavering.

He grinned again and shrugged. "Can't say I didn't try to change your mind."

She laughed throatily. "Now, that's a fact!"

He rose from his chair, hesitated for a moment, then turned back to her. "Ah . . . would you do me one last favor?"

"Certainly, Mr. Madison."

He fixed her with a warning gaze.

"Certainly, Jeffrey," she corrected herself. "What is it?"

"Would you cancel my reservations? I hate to sight-see alone."

"What?" She rose halfway from her Queen Anne chair.

His large hand pressed her shoulder, easing her back into place. "Temper, temper!"

Trying to catch her breath, she used vast amounts of energy to harness an unladylike retort. "You're perfectly right. Thank you, sir. I'll see to it at once."

He grinned like a young kid who'd just pulled his best practical joke of the week. He was delighted with her iron control. It was a little ragged around the edges, but she'd done it.

"See you around, Annie." He waved jauntily. "Thanks for your time. Oh," he added, "if you should change your mind, I'll be in the lounge on Friday evening. Perhaps you'll let me buy you a drink."

She glared after him as he walked away, then her irritation began to fade as she saw the humor of the situation. "What chutzpah!" she exclaimed softly. The man simply would not take no for an answer.

She saw Jeffrey again later in the afternoon, but

he didn't look her way. Dressed in sports clothes, he strode out the front entrance and got into her boss's limousine. Mrs. Cummings's chauffeur, Charles, was at the wheel. Ann could see Jeffrey speak with him for a moment, then the limo pulled away. Did Jeffrey know her boss? she wondered. It certainly was curious that he should be using her car. And her chauffeur.

Two

Thursday's assignment for Ann was the kitchen, and it was an eye-opener. No wonder this hotel was a world-class establishment, she thought, watching the chief chef and his many assistants prepare sumptuous individual meals for scores of room-service orders.

Ann's job was general gofer—scrub the carrots, shave the imported cheeses, separate the large green beans from the smaller, more tender ones—for Karl, the vegetable chef. At ten-thirty he told her it was time for her fifteen-minute break.

"R-r-ouse mit du!"

She laughed when he waved a spoon in the air, shooing her outside. Inhaling deeply, she relaxed on a low stone wall, watching the clouds change shape in the gentle breeze.

"Hi, Ms. Ann. Want some company?"

27

She turned and grinned at the gray-haired man walking toward her. "Charles! Come on, join me." She scooted over. "Hear from the boss?"

"Yes. She hopes to be home by tomorrow."

"I'll bet you're glad."

He nodded. "I haven't had enough to do."

Ann thought this might be an opportune moment to ask the question that had been burning in her mind since yesterday. "Charles, do you know Jeffrey Madison?"

Charles studied her for a moment before he answered. "I've been driving him a little. Why do you ask?"

She shrugged and smoothed wrinkles from her white kitchen dress. "I saw you drive away with him yesterday afternoon . . . and I wondered how come. Is he a friend of the family?"

"Mrs. Cummings told me I could take some outside jobs if I wanted," he explained. "To earn a little extra cash while she was away." He grinned. "Fine woman, Mrs. Cummings."

Ann agreed, then shared the amusing tale of Jeffrey's canceled tours. "I thought I was going to crown him."

"I've felt the same way at times."

She groaned in commiseration. "Don't tell me he made *you* his tour guide?"

Charles shook his head, gazing over the landscaped grounds. "I only took him to the golf course. He and Mr. Bailey played eighteen holes. Today I have to take him back with Ms. Wickoff." He shook his head. "That man must be fresh out of golfing partners.

Everyone on the management staff plays with a big handicap."

Ann frowned in concern. Tom Bailey was the hotel's public relations director and Carol Wickoff was the convention coordinator. Could Jeffrey Madison be headhunting among the executives of the hotel? She decided she'd better watch him closely during the next few days.

Just then Karl bellowed from the kitchen door, and she rose quickly. "Looks as if there's no rest for the wicked."

Charles grinned. "That goes for the good ones too, little lady. Don't you work too hard."

Ann was crossing the lobby while on her lunch break on Friday, and she saw Jeffrey leave the hotel with Mark Ludlow, the general manager. The two appeared to be in fine spirits. Those golfing expeditions between Jeffrey and management were not happening by accident, she thought, and picked up a phone to call her boss.

"Come right up," Vanessa said. "I've been home for hours."

Within five minutes Ann was in the penthouse on the twelfth floor of the hotel.

"Hello, Mrs. Cummings," she greeted her boss. "You look wonderfully rested."

Vanessa smoothed her newly coiffed ash-blond hair, then motioned her protégée to a burgundy leather chair. "I'll certainly be relieved when you finish your assignment, Ann." She fluttered her perfectly manicured fingertips over her desk. "I'm getting buried under all this paper."

"I could help you after hours, Mrs. Cummings," Ann offered.

"Oh, darling, I'm just a complaining old woman," Vanessa said, laughing at herself.

"You just got out of a sick bed," Ann said, "but you're certainly not old."

Vanessa speared her with an unwavering gaze. "Just how old am I, Ann?"

"Forty-five . . . *maybe*," Ann said, praying she hadn't guessed too high.

Vanessa leaned back in her chair and laughed merrily. "Pierre, my exercise coach, will be delighted."

Ann began to breathe again, then shifted uncomfortably as Vanessa studied her closely.

"You're concerned about something," Vanessa finally said. "All right, out with it." Her eyes narrowed and she placed one hand on her chest. "Don't tell me you're going to renege on our bargain."

"Me, ma'am? Not on your life!" Ann exclaimed, sitting up straight. "This is where I belong."

Vanessa inhaled deeply. "I couldn't agree with you more. Well, then. What?"

"I really hate to burden you at this time," Ann said evasively. "Just when you've arrived home from the hospital."

"Oh, pish-posh, child! Tell me."

Ann spent the next few minutes explaining her concerns about a man named Jeffrey Madison. She told Vanessa about his outings with each of the three leading executives of the hotel, verifying her observation with Charles's information.

"Each was obviously planned, Mrs. Cummings."

"I wonder what the man does for a living?"

"He told me he's a headhunter . . . for corporate executives."

Vanessa cleared her throat and leaned forward in her chair. "Mmmm, you seem to know a good bit about him."

It took Ann another fifteen minutes to tell her boss all that had happened in the past few days. By the end of Ann's recitation, Vanessa was gasping with laughter.

"None of it was very funny at the time," Ann muttered.

"Priceless!" Vanessa spun around in her desk chair, clapping her hands together, then wiped tears from her sparkling eyes. "Absolutely outrageous!"

"Yes, ma'am." Though Ann was glad she was entertaining her boss, she wished Vanessa could have taken her place during some of the episodes with Jeffrey. Except when he'd kissed her hand, she qualified. She rubbed her tingling fingertips over her skirt and concentrated again on the conversation. "So where does that leave the headhunting Mr. Madison?" she asked.

"Right where he belongs. Here."

"You're not going to order him to leave?" Ann asked incredulously.

Vanessa bounced up from her chair and began to pace rapidly across the thick beige carpet. "If we tell him to leave, he'll still be working, only we won't be able to keep track of him."

Ann followed her boss's movements, feeling as if she were watching a one-woman tennis match. "I'm afraid I don't quite understand."

Vanessa moved to Ann's chair so quickly, she made the younger woman jump. "You must be my ears and eyes, Ann."

"But the hotel rules . . ."

"Forget them!" she declared breezily, waving her hand in regal dismissal. "This is a special assignment. What will I do if this renegade shanghais my key people?"

Ann's gaze was captured by Vanessa's entreating eyes. Without her boss having to say another word, Ann could tell she was begging her not to let the River Regency down.

"I'll do it," she promised, taking Vanessa's proffered hand to seal the bargain. "I won't fail you, Mrs. Cummings. I promise. My future lies with the River Regency now."

"Truer words were never spoken, Ann. Now I expect you've other duties to attend to, so I'll let you get to them. But remember, dear, watch that man's every move, and keep me apprised of the situation."

Friday evening, after dinner, Ann prepared for her special assignment . . . although she had trouble remembering that this *was* an assignment, and not a secret assignation with a wonderfully compelling man. She indulged in a long, fragrant bubble bath, then chose a new gown she'd purchased the week before at the Josephina Boutique in the Galleria. It was a figure-skimming French creation of blue silk. A simple but bold design, it draped over her right shoulder, leaving her left one bare, and caressed her legs at mid-calf in an uneven hem.

She brushed her sable hair until it shone, then fastened it behind her ear with an iridescent indigo butterfly clip. Tiny pearls graced her ears; a single pearl on a gossamer-thin chain encircled her wrist, and another hugged her ankle.

She leaned close to the mirror to inspect her makeup. Her teal blue shadow made her eyes appear even larger and bluer. She smiled confidently at her reflection. She looked like an entirely different person tonight, with her hair cascading to her slender waist and one shoulder bare. Gone for tonight was the trim, serious professional. The woman who'd taken her place was mysterious, alluring.

Ann felt lighthearted and relaxed . . . and excited. Something exciting was going to happen to her this evening. She could sense it.

Stop dreaming, Annie, she told herself. She had a job to do tonight. Her boss was counting on her.

When she slipped on her silver high-heeled sandals, she felt again the stir of excitement, and laughed. Her heart beat a little faster, and her cheeks flushed as she realized the risks of this challenge. Vanessa hadn't set down any rules.

She'd only told Ann to watch Jeffrey Madison like a hawk.

Ann dabbed a sultry perfume on her pulse points and behind her knees, then picked up her lamé handbag. Watching Jeffrey would be her pleasure, she thought as she took one last look in the mirror. He was one of the most handsome and strong men she'd ever had the privilege to meet. He had a zany sense of humor, not unlike her own. And he seemed to be a gambler too. Didn't he risk his life to rescue little boys from scary mountaintops? She shook a finger at her reflection. That kind of thinking could get her in way over her head.

Downstairs she strolled toward the garden lounge, pausing by the shimmering fountain in the lobby. The bubbling water cascaded over a tall crystal sculpture whose slim shape reminded Ann of a futuristic, contoured obelisk. Underwater spotlights gave the clear glass a mysterious aura.

She ordered a glass of champagne to celebrate the end of her first week at the hotel. She was about to sit at a table in the lounge, when she heard the first notes of a melody drift across the lobby from the grand piano. She glanced at her small gold watch. It was long past the hour when the house musicians entertained, so it must be one of the guests playing. She felt drawn to the enchanting sound and, champagne in hand, walked over to a large white sofa near the piano and sat down.

Jeffrey was playing the piano, and his attention was captured by the dark-haired woman in the blue dress. As he automatically played a popular

Gershwin tune, he tried to figure out the beautiful woman's identity. Was she who he thought she was?

She had a figure no man could forget, especially when it was encased in such an elegant but revealing dress. Though her face was shadowed, her long black hair seemed to shimmer. Spectacular was the only adjective that did it justice.

Look at me! he ordered silently, and as if she had read his mind, the woman gazed directly at him.

Yes! he thought, surprised at the intensity of his pleasure. It was Ann. He smiled broadly at her, holding her gaze while he improvised variations on romantic Broadway ballads. His mind was spinning dizzily. He was absolutely stunned by Ann's beauty. She was totally different tonight. Her dress, her hair, even the relaxed way she was sitting. It was as if she were a stranger, though he knew that she was not.

Still, the idea lingered, making Jeffrey more determined than ever to know the elusive Ms. Waverly on a more personal level. To that purpose, he began a medley of tunes dedicated to her blue gown, her indigo-blue eyes, and *his* blue mood if he were rebuffed again.

Ann had recognized Jeffrey as soon as he'd smiled at her. He looked magnificent in a midnight-blue raw silk jacket, and his sun-streaked blond hair gleamed in the soft lights. She was pleased she could elicit such attention from the most handsome man in the lobby. She could tell he hadn't realized who she was at first, and that thought made her smile.

She settled back against the cushions, crossing her long legs, and lifted her glass in a silent toast to his talent.

Captivated by her smile, Jeffrey felt a rush of heat through his body. His attraction to her was affecting him . . . dramatically. His pulse was racing and every muscle in his body seemed to be tautening with excitement. Was it, he asked himself, because she seemed approachable tonight? Her smile was sensuous and mysterious, provocative yet sincere. What message was she sending him? he wondered, intrigued by the possibilities.

At that moment a tall, debonair man approached Ann. He sat on the black marble table beside the sofa and began talking with her. Jeffrey glared at the man, then abruptly ended the song he was playing and walked over to Ann. He sat down beside her, patently ignoring the intruder.

"I hope you enjoyed the music, darling," he said, stroking her upper arm. "I played the medley especially for you."

Jeffrey's tingling touch sent a secret message directly to Ann's center. She could feel her breasts firm, the tips pucker. Mesmerized, she said, "I loved every note, darling. Thank you."

The other man took the hint, bid Ann a pleasant good evening, and retreated to the lounge. Jeffrey couldn't hide his self-satisfied grin.

"I wasn't absolutely sure it was you at first," he said to Ann.

She laughed softly, gazing at him through the

thick veil of her long dark lashes. "Do you make a habit of seducing women with your beautiful music?"

"Only the most attractive ones. Tell me," he murmured, "was I successful?"

Oh, that voice! she thought, feeling waves of pleasure ripple up from her toes. Why couldn't he sound like a foghorn . . . or how Valentino really sounded, high and squeaky? It seemed so unfair. Smiling demurely, she traced the edge of her glass with one fingertip, coaxing a musical tone from the smooth crystal. "Perhaps."

Encouraged, Jeffrey moved closer. He breathed in deeply, savoring her heady, tantalizing fragrance. "I'm very glad you came tonight. May I assume that you've changed your mind?"

He was still stroking her arm and she caught his hand in hers, halting his exploration. His touch was doing more than he realized, gradually turning her middle to Jell-O. Or *did* he know? she mused, giving him a mysterious smile. "It isn't wise to assume anything these days, Jeffrey."

"Especially with you?"

"You're very astute."

"And you're pointedly vague," he complained softly. "You've been constantly in my thoughts today. The man on security duty in the lobby asked me three times if he could help me."

Ann tipped her head questioningly.

He chuckled. "I was looking for you, but I think the guy thought I was casing the joint."

She laughed and patted his hand. "Poor baby. I'm sorry Tim gave you a bad time."

"None of it matters, Ann, if you'll go out with me." He stared into her indigo eyes. "Will you? I want so much to be with you."

The warm glow in his eyes, the seductive note in his voice, almost made her forget entirely about his job, his golf games with River Regency executives. She inhaled his individual scent combined with some wonderfully masculine cologne, then nodded her head, sending strands of sable hair shimmering across her blue bodice.

"Yes, Jeffrey. I want to be with you too," she said. And it had nothing to do with her assignment for Vanessa, she realized. "But we'll have to be very discreet. I could be fired on the spot if we're discovered."

His hand tightened around hers, then began a seductive caressing that caused her to shiver. "I'm very glad you changed your mind," he said. "I want us to be friends . . . *good* friends."

She laughed throatily, relieving the tension in her body. When they exchanged secretive smiles, she felt almost light-headed. At that moment she wished she'd never gone to Vanessa Cummings with her suspicions. Jeffrey Madison might be an executive recruiter, but her intuition told her he would never do anything unethical. Still, her good sense demanded to be heard. Then why had he convinced her, it asked, to break house rules? She gave her head a little shake. The answer was simple. He liked her. Could he help it if she worked where he was staying?

"I think we're going to have to find a more private

place, don't you?" she said. "The River Regency lobby presents a rather panoramic view of our budding friendship."

He took the fragile glass from her and placed it on the table, then rose smoothly, drawing her up with him. "We'll take a stroll," he said. "Eventually we'll find our way to the side terrace. Its shadows will give us the privacy we seek." He tucked her arm in his. "Come, my lady. We begin our adventure."

"Do you think we can really fool the world, even for a little while?" she asked, her stomach clenching with sudden apprehension. And could she fool him as well? she wondered. Her conscience gave her a decidedly sharp nudge and added, Did she want to? Spying was about as foreign to her usually forth-right way of living as hundred-year-old brandy was to apple pie. Why had she given her promise to her boss? She liked Jeffrey. She wanted to know him better too. But now her role as informant would get in the way of any honest relationship they might pursue. "Suddenly I have cold feet," she whispered.

"When the rules of the world are foolish, we break them," he said, his smile assured. "Or at least we bend them to our liking."

"But this rule makes sense, Jeffrey. I think I may be asking for trouble." If she could convince him of her hesitancy, perhaps he'd understand. How could she do this? She didn't want to spy on him. She'd never knowingly deceived anyone in her life, and it didn't sit well with her.

"It makes no sense where you and I are concerned," he said. "And I'll give you no trouble . . . *if* you start walking toward the terrace this instant." His blue eyes grew dark as he met her wavering gaze. "Come on," he challenged her, grinning devilishly. "I thought you were a gambler."

She laughed, tipping her head to the side. Oh, she did want to go with him, she thought. Perhaps her worrying was all for nothing. For tonight, she'd just go with the flow. "You've just said the magic word, Mr. Madison, but I've never seen such staggering odds—against me."

He led her across the lobby, firmly holding her arm. "I rather think this time, the odds are against the house."

When they'd arrived on the starlit terrace, they stood quietly for a long moment, savoring the fresh breeze, gazing at the shadowed branches woven with moonbeams. They could almost taste the exquisite fragrance of the flowers. It was a night made for romance, Jeffrey thought, but first, he and Ann needed to talk.

"How long have you been in St. Charles?" he asked.

"Less than a month," she answered. She told him how she'd decided to leave Chicago and come south while still remaining in the Midwest. "I'm from a little town called Weir, on the Kansas-Missouri border. My parents still live there. Mom's a bank teller, and Dad's a trucker." She grinned. "And before you ask, yes, every high school game we ever played was filled with cheers about the *Weir-d* students from Weir, Kansas."

"A man would have to be blind to think it's true," Jeffrey said. "You're breathtakingly beautiful, Ann."

She felt his arms steal around her waist, drawing her against his body. "Tell me about your home," she said, hoping to keep the conversation alive.

"Mountainview is a lovely village built in the clouds."

"It sounds wonderful."

"It's spectacular," he murmured against her ear. His warm breath made goose bumps rise on her sensitized skin. "But you'd outshine the snow-capped vista."

He nestled his cheek against her hair. His caressing words, his gentle touch, melted Ann's reserve. She tilted her head to the side, providing him easy access to the velvety skin of her neck. His lips explored leisurely, dwelling finally over the rapid pulse at the base of her neck.

"Are you free tomorrow?" he asked as his lips strayed to her bare shoulder.

"Mmmm," she answered, breathless from his touch. "I'm off for the weekend."

"I want to go far, far away from this place. In the country. Out of doors. Where we can be alone. Do you know of such a place, my lovely?"

"Yes," she answered on a sigh. "But it may be too primitive for your taste."

He chuckled. "Ann, that's about as funny as your offer to book me at the Lasta Motel." He pulled her tight against his body. "Feel my response to you, woman. I'd say your choice is perfect. I'm feeling decidedly primitive right now."

She strained against his hold. "*Right now* we have

to make plans, Jeffrey. I can't afford to be discovered by anyone on the staff."

He relaxed his grip so she was more comfortable but didn't release her. They carefully planned their escape for the next day, where they could secretly rendezvous. When every detail was settled to Ann's satisfaction, she smiled, her eyes dancing with excitement. "We'll have a wonderful day together. I think it'll be warm enough to swim in the creek."

"Is that a pointed suggestion that I bring along my bathing suit?" he asked. He lifted her left hand to his lips and kissed her palm, sweeping his tongue across the heart line.

"You'd better," she said, laughing even as she shivered from his erotic caress. "My little hideaway may be primitive, but it's not *that* primitive."

"I'll be discreet," he promised.

"I hope so." She hesitated, and her gaze shifted away from him. "Can you get into trouble over this too?" she asked softly, suddenly afraid he had a fiancée. Or a wife!

He sensed her withdrawal instantly. "I'm not involved with another woman, Ann. I'm not attached in any way."

Her sigh was quiet, but still audible.

"You know what the best part of this is going to be?" he asked. "When we win, we get to share the payoff equally."

She trembled, knowing exactly what he hoped that payoff would be. Easing away from his embrace, she looked into his shadowed eyes and smiled bemusedly. "I'm not sure I'm ready for such high stakes," she confessed. "And now I'm going to get some sleep."

"I'll walk you to your door."

She shook her head, and the light sparkled in her dark hair. "I don't think that would be wise, Jeffrey."

"Then I'll kiss you good night here."

Without another word he drew her back into his embrace. Shyly she allowed her slender arms to curve around his shoulders, and he pulled her close, molding her firm breasts to his chest. His lips brushed softly across hers. He explored the fullness of her lower lip, placed small, tender kisses at the corners of her mouth, outlined the shape of both her lips with the tip of his tongue.

Fascinated by the feel of his mouth on hers, Ann parted her lips on a sigh. At once Jeffrey deepened the kiss, sweeping his tongue into her dark warmth. With firm strokes he tasted her, rubbing against the smooth sides of her tongue, then lingering for a long moment until she joined in the dance.

Time stood still. A gentle breeze caressed her flushed skin as his callused hands played along her back, drawing her closer, letting her know how their kiss had aroused him. She was intoxicated by the feel, the taste of him, and her hands crept to the back of his head, pressing his mouth hard against hers. His own hands threaded through her long hair, slowly wrapping themselves in it until her head fell back, exposing the vulnerable ivory skin of her throat. He trailed kisses across her cheek, slipped below her jawline to tantalize the pulse point there before his lips burned along her shoulder, then returned to her mouth.

Ann was overcome by pleasure. Jeffrey's kiss—if one rated such things—deserved four stars. And if his look of surprised delight when they ended the kiss and simply gazed at each other was any indication, he, too, was taken aback by the potency of their attraction.

"I had no idea," he said hoarsely.

She had to smile at his words. One would think he'd never kissed a woman before. She sighed, realizing that she had never been kissed like that before.

"I honestly had no idea," he repeated, still looking somewhat dazed.

"I did," she said saucily. "Why do you think I tried to stay away? I never lay odds on a sure thing."

"You're a brave little angel, Annie."

"No, Jeffrey. You've got that all wrong. It's 'Fools rush in where . . .' Well, you know how it goes."

"Do you really think we're being foolish?" he asked, tightening his hold on her.

"How do I know?" She brushed a golden curl off his forehead and sighed. "I'm still feeling the aftershocks."

"Me too." His smoky eyes narrowed and his mouth curved into a comical leer. "Wanna try for a seven on the Richter scale?"

"I'm not that brave," she said, shaking her head and gently extricating herself from his embrace. "I'll see you tomorrow morning. I hope you can find our meeting place."

"I'll find it," he said firmly. "Kiss me once more, love."

"Uh-uh!" She backed away. "If I do, I'll never find my room."

"I won't sleep tonight anyway." His gaze traced every curve of her body. "You can bet on it."

The obvious passion in his voice and words urged her to return to his arms, but fortunately she had regained some control over herself. She murmured, "Good night," and started walking toward the door. Then she paused and turned back to him. "Jeffrey?"

"Yes?"

"Be sure to bring along old sneakers tomorrow. The creek bed has some sharp rocks and we don't want you to cut your foot . . . again!"

"What the . . . ? How do you . . ."

Laughing softly, she disappeared into the hotel.

Three

Ann thought she'd never seen a more glorious Saturday morning. Dressed in a peach terry romper with a matching scarf pulling her hair back in a ponytail, she was filled with anticipation as she entered the hotel kitchen to pick up the picnic basket she'd ordered late the night before.

"*Ach*, you look bee-u-ti-ful, *mein Kind*," exclaimed Karl, giving her a paternal pat on her shoulder. "If I were only twenty years younger." He sighed, his eyes twinkling merrily.

"You'd fall in love with your wife all over again," Ann said, giving him a quick peck on one rosy cheek. "Remember, you adore blondes."

"But a brunette such as you might tempt me, Anna."

"Better not let Helga hear you say that," she said playfully. Glancing around, she spotted a wicker basket on one of the side tables. "Is that my picnic, Karl?"

"*Ja.* I packed it myself, and added a few surprises too."

"I love surprises. Thank you." She slipped her arm through the handle and walked out of the kitchen, heading for her car.

She placed the heavy basket and her canvas tote bag in the trunk of her vintage Corvette convertible, then pulled out of the hotel parking garage. About three miles down the road was the Muddy River Shopping Mall, and she parked in front of the post office. Jeffrey was leaning against the flagpole. She waved to him, then watched as he strolled toward her car.

He looked relaxed, assured, and darned sexy! she thought as her heart did a little double beat. The hair on his tanned muscular legs reflected gold in the sunlight. His hands were thrust into the pockets of faded cutoffs, drawing her attention to his narrow hips, and his knit shirt emphasized his broad chest and wide shoulders. On top of everything else the color of his shirt perfectly matched his sky-blue eyes.

Oh, yes, Ann thought as he winked at her. The man was a menace to her emotional stability. But to be honest, she liked what his nearness did to her. It made her blood bubble in her veins as if she'd been drinking champagne. Then, once again, with no warning, her conscience burst her effervescent mood. She was supposed to be spying on Jeffrey, not enjoying his company. Damn!

"Hi, Annie," he said when he reached the car. He tossed his worn knapsack into the backseat, then placed his hands on her door and leaned down so that his face was level with hers. "It's good to see you this morning." His casual caress of her cheek didn't prepare her for the jolt she felt the next moment when he brushed a tender kiss across her parted lips. "You look like orange sherbet in that outfit. Cool, refreshing. Gorgeous."

My, my, my! purred Ann's heart. Even in broad daylight Jeffrey Madison had a wonderful voice. He would have made a fabulous late night disc jockey. "Hi, Jeff," she said, feeling breathless. "I'm glad you didn't get lost."

"Fat chance! Didn't you know this was the only mall in town? The taxi driver thought I was a little nuts when I gave him such detailed instructions for getting here."

Ann's cheeks colored and she lowered thick lashes over dancing blue eyes. "I knew. I just didn't want to take any chances."

He bent to kiss her again, this time lingeringly. "You say the nicest things, Ms. Waverly." He planted a kiss on the tip of her nose, then strode around the front of the car to the passenger side.

"Love your car, Annie," he said as he slid into the passenger seat. He smoothed his hand over the supple leather upholstery. "I might have known you'd drive something like this. A red Classic convertible with a white interior. All in mint condition." He took her hand and brought it to his lips, kissing her fingertips as he gazed at her. "A gambler's car."

"Why do you say that?" she asked softly. His kisses had distracted her, and she could barely pull her thoughts together to follow the conversation. "Red's my favorite color."

"Cops get a kick out of chasing beautiful women driving fast little red cars."

"They go after *blondes*, not brunettes." As he continued to caress her hand and smiled at her, she shrugged and added, "I hedge my bets with a fuzz buster."

"Smart girl."

The sun beat down on their uncovered heads as Ann drove along Old River Road toward her most recently discovered favorite spot in the world. Jeffrey amused himself by untying her scarf, then slipping off the elastic band that held her hair and threading his fingers through the wind-whipped mane.

"Your hair is like silk, Ann. I love to watch it dance in the breeze."

She laughed. "You won't think it's so silky when I make you brush out all the snarls."

"Yes, I will," he said softly. "And you won't have to make me do a thing. I'm looking forward to it."

She shook her head, wondering what had happened to make him such an obliging fellow today. She guessed his dancing eyes would grow cold if he knew the secret reason that they were together. And once again she wondered why she'd made such an insane promise to her boss. Well, she thought, she was going to have to make the best of it. A promise was a promise.

"You'll have an opportunity to do just that as soon as we get to where we're going," she said.

"Is it much farther?"

"Another five minutes or so before we leave the highway."

Jeffrey was singing along in a strong bass voice to a song on the car stereo when she turned onto a gravel road. She drove cautiously for about a mile before she slowed the car to a stop.

Straightening, Jeffrey pushed his aviator sunglasses down his nose and stared at the thick, tangled underbrush on both sides of the road. He groaned. "Annie, please don't tell me this is your primitive place."

Her laughter startled a flock of blackbirds roosting in a stand of tall cottonwood trees. Their raucous cawing echoed through the woods.

"No," she said. "This is where the entrance to my primitive place is hidden." She hopped out of the car and jogged to a vine-covered gate at the edge of the thicket. She pushed it open and drove through. Jeffrey closed it again. "You're sworn to secrecy," she said as they continued down a dirt road. "I signed a one-year lease on a few acres down by the river when I got my new job here. I think the owner might be a hermit. He lives alone and generally doesn't seem to like outsiders. Anyway, no one knows about it but him and me . . . and now, you."

"I know how to keep a secret," Jeffrey assured her, then his mouth curved in a boyish grin. "You say you've never brought anyone else here?"

"Not another soul."

"Now I really feel special." He ran a finger down her cheek. "You trust me."

"Sure, I do," she said, giving him a sidelong glance.

He squinted at her. "Have I missed something? We are going to be alone, aren't we?"

"Of course we are. Just you and me and my CB."

"Hedging your bet again, huh?"

She didn't answer. Instead, she pressed down on the accelerator and they shot along the dirt road—around mudholes and over rough areas that resembled washboards. Just when Jeffrey thought either the car's bottom or his was going to shake loose, Ann drove into a tiny meadow secluded from the world and nestled near the bank of a stream.

She stopped the car and they both climbed out. In the distance they heard the solo cadenza of the tumbling water, the harmonious songs of a meadowlark and a cardinal. Nearby was the rhythmic drone of industrious honeybees. Jeffrey caught Ann's hand in his and blinked, hardly believing his eyes.

Long tender grasses wafted gently in the moist breeze. Black-eyed Susans and bluebells and buttercups nodded a mute hello. Purple thistle and lavender crown vetch vied for attention with exquisite Queen Anne's lace. In the far corner a small patch of sunflowers stood like stately sentinels, guarding the path that wound through the basswood trees to the noisy brook.

Finally Jeffrey drew in a long breath. "Am I dreaming?"

"Want me to pinch you?" Ann offered, stroking the golden hair on his forearm.

"Uh-uh. You're too eager." He chuckled, and captured her from behind, slipping his arms around her waist. "But it's breathtaking, Ann. It's like stepping into another world."

She smoothed her hands along his arms, delighted that he liked her special place. "Are you glad you came today?"

"I wouldn't want to be anyplace else . . . except perhaps my mountain retreat. But then, you wouldn't be there with me. Tell me, how can a trainee afford to lease even a few acres of paradise?"

"This is undeveloped land. Who'd want it? In these parts it's dirt cheap."

"And no one knows it's here?"

She shook her head, absentmindedly tucking a long strand of hair behind her ear. "Oh, I suppose the Indians knew about it once." Her voice became dreamy. "I like to imagine that they used this spot for a resting place before they traveled farther downriver to the fur-trading post. It would have been safe here, with water to drink, fish and game and wild berries to eat, and plenty of wood for their fires."

She sighed contentedly. "Sometimes, after I've swum in the creek, I fall asleep in the sunshine. Then I dream about how it might have been a hundred years ago."

"And do you dream of a handsome brave?" Jeffrey asked, drawing her closer, nuzzling his cheek against her hair.

Relaxing against his strong body, she sighed and closed her eyes, saying nothing.

"Do you?" he prodded, kissing the sensitive cord along her neck.

"Sometimes."

"And does he also swim with you?"

Jeffrey's sensuous voice, his hot breath washing across her skin, started a primal message pulsating within her body. She could feel heat rise inside her loins, and she trembled. In another moment Jeffrey was going to kiss her. Though she wanted him to, she knew it wouldn't be wise. She felt out of control already. And then what would she do?

"Does he swim with you?" Jeffrey asked again, trying to ignore the stiffening of Ann's body. She was getting ready to change the subject, he guessed, bracing himself for her next move. He wasn't disappointed.

"He swims with me only *after* he's brushed the snarls from my hair so I can braid it," she said, gently pulling out of Jeffrey's arms. "Shall we get the blanket and my tote bag from the trunk of the car so we can sit while you work?"

"By all means."

They spread out the blanket and sat down, then Ann handed Jeffrey her brush and comb. He began to comb through the tangled hair, taking care not to pull too hard and hurt her scalp. When the hair was all smooth and shining, he brushed it through, singing softly. "I dream of Annie with her long dark hair . . ."

Ann was almost asleep, thanks to his gentle ministering and the warm sun. She smiled dreamily when her head lolled to the side and was steadied by his large, capable hands. "You have a beautiful voice, Jeff. And you have gentle hands."

He eased her into his arms, continuing his massage of her scalp and nape. "Thank you, love."

"Mmmm," she mumbled sleepily.

"I'm going to kiss you now. Tenderly."

"Tenderly?"

"Yes." He covered her mouth with his, inhaling the fragrance of spice and wildflowers in her hair. He felt as if he'd stumbled into a mystical glen and found the lovely Sleeping Beauty. Ann moaned softly when he traced her pliant lips with the tip of his tongue, coaxing her to open to him. She complied and he slipped within, savoring her essence, exploring her warmth, her satiny smoothness. He tightened his embrace, and her voluptuous breasts pressed against his chest. One of her arms circled his waist while the other slid along his shoulder so she could play with the thick hair curling over the back of his collar.

He groaned when she responded to his kiss, joining him in the dancing duel. Her hand tugged his shirttail from his shorts and crept inside. She traced his spine, each vertebra, every straining muscle, counting the ripples of his lower ribs.

Her hand slipped beneath his arm and wandered through the soft curls on his chest, and he sucked in his breath, tightening his hold on her. When her fingers grazed across his hard nipples, she discovered how much her touch could affect his breathing. He shuddered in her arms, his own hand gliding roughly down her back to massage and knead her derriere.

His touch was sure, Ann thought, and heavenly. Heavenly and right. Sighing, she snuggled against him, prepared to stay for a while. But the kiss ended abruptly when they both heard the crackle of broken twigs some distance behind them. They pulled away from each other and turned toward the sound. Their heavy breathing almost drowned out the steadily approaching footfalls in the woods.

"I thought you said no one knew about this place," Jeffrey said.

"No one does, except Ezra."

"The hermit?"

"Yes." She scrambled to her feet, and had to grab on to Jeffrey's shoulder when her legs at first refused to support her. "He's come by to say hello a time or two."

Just then a bearded man dressed in well-worn jeans and a black T-shirt emblazoned with *WOOD-STOCK* stepped out of the shadows at the edge of the woods. His dark eyes were barely visible beneath the wide brim of his battered bead-banded straw hat. He didn't move but only stood there, watching, waiting.

"Hello, Ezra," Ann called, waving cheerfully.

" 'Lo, Annie," he said, touching the front of his hat but never taking his eyes off Jeffrey. "You all right?"

She laughed nervously and glanced at Jeffrey. He was staring back at Ezra, his body tense.

"I'm fine, Ezra. And you?"

"Fine. Who's the stranger?"

"A friend, Ezra."

"You sure?"

What was going on here? she wondered distract-edly. *Both* men were acting strangely. Sniffing the air, glaring at each other, as if they were getting ready to fight. Over her? Good Lord, they were pre-pared to do battle in order to protect her, she real-ized, and she knew she had to put a stop to it at once.

"Sure, I'm sure. Let me introduce you." She took Jeffrey's hand and led him over to Ezra. "Jeffrey meet Ezra, my friend and landlord. Ezra meet Jef-frey, a friend from Mountainview, Utah."

She watched, fascinated, while the two men sized up each other, then sighed with relief when Ezra finally stuck out his large hand, and they shook hands.

"Live in the mountains, do ya?" Ezra asked.

"Yup."

"Hunt?"

"Only for food."

"Trap?"

"I'd rather not, but I know how."

"Track?"

"I learned from one of the best."

"What ya doin' out here?"

"Can't breathe in the city."

"Me neither." Ezra nodded once, then turned toward Ann. "Ya got yourself a good man here, Annie."

"Yeah?" She watched Jeffrey draw in a deep breath as if he were particularly proud that he'd passed muster with Ezra. Men! she thought, grinning. They had such strange rites. "How can you tell, Ezra?"

"I trust him. He doesn't talk much, and he'll die if he doesn't stay near the land."

"Well, thanks for your opinion, Ezra. Would you like to stay and eat with us?"

Shifting his gaze back to Jeffrey, Ezra touched his hat brim again and grinned quickly. "Thanks just the same, Ann, but you best eat your full ration today." He locked eyes with Jeffrey for another instant, then winked. "I've got a notion you're gonna need all your strength to handle this here mountain man."

"Wanna bet?"

"I never bet on sure things, Annie."

"Well," she said, determined to have the last word, "at least he's not *my* mountain man."

Ezra took one more look at Jeffrey, then cocked his head to the side when Jeffrey's mouth lifted in a confident grin. "Wanna bet?"

He was gone before Ann could fire a comeback.

"That man's been out in the woods too long," she complained, flabbergasted that he'd disappeared so quickly.

"No, he hasn't," Jeffrey said, leading her back to the blanket. They sat down again. "He knows what's important, that's all."

"How did you learn all that stuff you two were talking about?" she asked, not moving when he began to brush her hair again. "Did you really learn to track from one of the best?"

"Sure did. My teacher was Thadius Gatberry, one of the last mountain men in Utah." He paused, momentarily distracted by the way the sunbeams wove golden threads through Ann's hair. "Thadius taught me the ways of the mountains, testing me, pushing me hard, so I'd keep breaking through to greater levels of endurance."

He sighed and looked off in the distance, remembering. "It was his training that saved my life during more than one dangerous adventure. I learned to trust my instincts, to live off the land, and to track. He said I was a natural."

Jeffrey idly stroked Ann's silken locks, reliving the two long days and nights of searching in the mountains before he'd flown to Missouri. "Time and time again, the skills Thadius taught me have saved other people's lives as well."

Ann turned to look at him. "The little boy that was lost?"

He nodded. "Yes."

"It was a shame you had to travel again before you could rest." Would he explain to her that important appointment he'd mentioned before? she wondered. Would he tell her anything she'd feel compelled to report to her boss? Damn, she hated this. She felt torn between her duty to Vanessa and her attraction to this man. Upset with herself because she couldn't make up her mind, she answered her own question.

"I guess you were able to sleep on the plane, though."

He chuckled as if at a private joke. "I could have slept, but it would have been a little tricky," he said.

He urged her to turn back around and tried his hand at braiding. "You see, I pilot my own plane."

She swiveled around and shook her head slowly. "Is there anything you can't do, Jeffrey Madison?"

"Yeah, I can't get you to sit still."

She turned her back to him and sat like a statue. Eventually she ruined her little act with a giggle.

"Share the humor?" Jeffrey asked.

"I was just thinking how closely connected your hobby is with your job."

He was instantly alert. "What do you mean?"

"Well, you hunt and track for fun and in serving the public, and you make your living by tracking down executives for jobs." She glanced over her shoulder and bit down on her lower lip to control her smile. "Or do you hunt jobs for executives?"

"Whatever," Jeffrey replied, concentrating on her braid and refusing to think what she'd have to say about his hobby if she knew about his *real* profession. The connection would give any psychologist fodder for a full year's analysis!

"You ought to write Thadius a thank-you letter," she said, "let him know you're a great success."

"I wish I could . . . but he's dead."

In one fluid motion she spun around and held his hands against her cheeks. "Oh, Jeff, I'm truly sorry. I didn't know. I wouldn't have made such a flip suggestion if I had."

"I know that," he said, bending to kiss her lips.

"Were you with him at the end?"

He nodded, then gazed off into the distance again. "When Thadius died, many people thought he was at least a hundred years old. He surely was a man of great wisdom and vast experience. I honored his last request and buried him beneath a lone pine just below the timberline on Murphy's Ridge." He paused, swallowing, and cleared his throat. "His grave is near the one-room log cabin he built and lived in for most of his life. It's mine now."

"Do you go there often?"

"Every chance I get. I go there for the solitude. I only live a few miles away, right on top of one of those grand mountains."

"It sounds as though you really love your home," she said.

He turned to meet her gaze. His answer was in his eyes even before he spoke. "Yes, Annie, I love the mountains. I don't ever want to live anywhere else. If a guy is lucky, he finds where he belongs early in life. He searches and searches and finally finds the one spot on earth where he's happy, content, able to commune with God and His creatures. I was one of the lucky ones. I know where I belong. In Mountainview."

"I went to the mountains once."

"Yeah? Which ones?"

"The Great Smoky Mountains. They really are great, you know."

"Mine are prettier by far. I'd like you to see them sometime. I'll bet you'd love them too."

She smiled. "I probably would. Love them, I mean. But only for a little while. Then I'd have to return to my real world."

"Don't tell me. Let me guess." He frowned and put

his fingertips to his temples. "Your world is the hotel business."

"Bingo! Give the man a teddy bear."

"You're really serious, aren't you? Don't you ever want a husband, a family?"

"Sure," she said, smiling at the thought. "But today a woman has the opportunity to do it all. Anyway, there's plenty of time for that. Right now I'm perfectly happy doing my job."

He played with a strand of her hair. "What if the man you love wants to, no, needs to live somewhere else . . . like on top of a mountain, for example? Could you change your mind?"

"It would depend."

"On what?"

Ann didn't like being pinned down, and this discussion had gone way off base as far as she was concerned. Jeffrey Madison might be the most attractive and compelling man she'd ever met, but she *had* known him only less than a week. "I don't know. I guess it would depend on how he and I could compromise. You know, work out a plan."

"In other words, you'd consider leaving the hotel business?"

She sat up straight. "Those aren't the words I would use."

"Well?"

"I want to stay in the hotel business. But my decision to stay at the River Regency for the rest of my natural life is not cast in stone. Now, is that a satisfactory answer to your question?"

"Yes, ma'am. You've answered just fine." He winked and grinned. "I like you, Annie Waverly."

She matched his grin, then laughed. "And I like you, Jeffie Madison."

"Damn, I wish old Thadius could have met you. He'd have given you a bear hug, I swear. And Thadius Gatberry was not a demonstrative man."

"But he must have been a wonderful man. After all, you loved him."

"Yes, I did. He honored friendship. Like Ezra does with you. That's why he reminded me of Thadius."

"He did?"

"Sure. Like Thadius, Ezra apparently believes man should live in the wild, eat off the land, make no trouble, but back down from no one."

He glanced at Ann, who had absentmindedly taken over the plaiting of her hair into a single long braid, and smiled. "Most important, a man must guard his woman against predators, especially the two-legged kind."

"Are you serious?"

"That's mountain law."

"Was that what you two were doing before I introduced you properly?"

"Yup."

She rolled her eyes. "Oh, please! Deliver me from men of few words."

He smiled charmingly and tipped an imaginary hat. "In the West, actions speak louder than words, ma'am."

"Wait! Don't tell me." She tapped her chin with an

index finger. "Ah . . . Gary Cooper," she said, point-
ing at him. "Right?"

"Nope."

"John Wayne?"

"Not even close."

She snapped her fingers. "I've got it. Cesar Romero."

He grimaced and shook his head. "Come on, wise
guy. Let's go swimming."

After their swim, Ann felt refreshed. She dried off
with her thick navy beach towel and passed it to
Jeffrey. Then she strode back to the car and hoisted
the picnic basket from the trunk. Jeffrey smoothed
the blanket, then kicked off his sloshing tennis
shoes and lay down on his side, propping his head
on his arm as he watched Ann walk back through
the meadow to him, carrying the basket. Just like
little Red Riding Hood, he thought. And he was the
big bad wolf. He liked the analogy, though he was
certain he much preferred Ann's red bikini over a
red hooded cloak.

He was so preoccupied with his thorough exami-
nation and appreciation of Ann's shapely figure, he
didn't realize she was practicing a little man-watching
herself. And Jeffrey was worth every bit of her attention, she decided. In his rather brief swim suit he
was magnificent!

"I've a basket filled with wonderful delights," she
said as she neared the blanket.

"I doubt anything in that basket could be more
wonderfully delightful than you," he said. "Annie?"

She set the basket down and knelt beside him on the blanket. "Yes?"

"I like you. Very much."

Her smile was shy, but she was obviously pleased. "I guess that makes us even," she said. She began to unload the basket, exclaiming as she uncovered each special dish Karl had prepared.

After eating their fill, Ann and Jeffrey lay side by side on their backs, watching fleecy clouds glide across the sky. They held hands but otherwise did not touch.

"Do you believe that feast?" Jeffrey said, sighing. "Croissants and veal, green grapes and Brie. Champagne."

"We won't discuss the fresh oysters and caviar," added Ann, laughing. "Price is no object when it comes to Karl's taste buds."

Jeffrey rolled onto his side. He traced her profile with one long finger. "You've got to admit, his dessert choice of dark and light Swiss chocolate brandy balls was inspired."

"Nothing of the kind," she said, trying not to look cross-eyed at his finger. "Karl just happens to know I'm a card-carrying chocoholic."

"Is that a fact?" Jeffrey murmured, preoccupied.

"Certifiable," she said, and grabbed his hand when he began to draw a line down the center of her body as well.

"Spoilsport," he whispered, rolling away from her but allowing her to keep hold of his hand.

She stroked the rough red scrapes on his knuckles, then clucked when she traced the spot where a fierce blister had formed and healed. "Did this all happen during the search?" she asked.

"Yes, I left so fast I forgot my heavier gloves. The pair I had came apart in no time. Tracking can be a very rough business."

"I'll tell you a secret." She smiled when he immediately moved back to her side and propped himself up so he could look into her eyes. "When I met you that first night, I thought you were so big and so strong. I figured you probably fought bears or wrestled mountain lions."

He chuckled. "I'm glad you think I'm big and strong, but I promise you I've never wrestled a mountain lion in my life. I'm not that brave."

She gazed into his sky-blue eyes, trying to tell him without words how proud she was of him. Realizing he would never understand her unspoken message, she brought his hand to her mouth and kissed the scars, the broken blisters, the half-healed cuts, mothering him.

"No," she murmured. She kissed each of his callused fingertips as she spoke. "You're not brave enough to battle wild animals with your bare hands. You're only brave enough to risk your life to rescue a frightened little boy off a treacherous mountain."

When he did not speak but just returned her gaze, she sat up and branded his palm with one more kiss. He reached for her, but she slipped away and scampered to the end of the blanket. "And now, my brave, brave man," she said, grabbing his left foot, "we need to discuss this other scar."

"Annie, I'm tickled to death that I'm your *anything*, but honey, I've got to warn you . . ."

She lifted her head and looked into his serious eyes.

"If you touch the bottom of my foot, I'll break your pretty little neck."

She began to giggle. "Did I just hear a Freudian slip of the lip, Jeffrey?" She laughed outright when she saw his look of panic.

"I get violent," he warned.

"You're ticklish!"

"Dammit, Annie, I can't control my reaction when someone touches the bottom of my feet."

She leaned down to peer closely at the crescent-shaped scar. Jeffrey wiggled his toes nervously, and when he tried to pull free, she held on tight.

"Ann, *don't!*"

"I won't . . . if you tell me how you got it."

"It's too damn embarrassing. I was just a little hotshot kid when it happened."

"I love little hotshot kid stories. Come on, Jeff. Let's hear it."

When he shook his head adamantly, she lifted one finger and began to make threatening circles above the white scar. Breathing harshly and making growling sounds, he tried to steel himself against her attack. His antics gave Ann a fit of giggles, which was her undoing. Lightning swift, he jerked his foot from her grasp, then spun around and threw himself on top of her, effectively turning the tables.

Ann blinked up at him, wondering how she had gotten there. It had all happened so quickly. He had her trapped and was savoring the moment. Grinning fiendishly, he held her hands above her head and began to kiss her. He explored her face, then investigated her neck and shoulders.

"And now, my lovely one," he said, still breathing heavily, but for another reason now, "since you've found my literal Achilles heel, I intend to find your figurative one." She stared up at him defiantly. "You may as well tell me. It's only a matter of time before I find it."

"I'll tell you if you tell me how you got that scar," she bartered.

He tipped his head to one side as if in deep contemplation. "Naw," he finally said, grinning. "It'll be more fun to find it myself." When she didn't move a muscle, no matter how he prodded her ribs, he deduced the spot must be below the waist. "Where is it?" he asked. "The hips? Your knees?"

She couldn't control the involuntary jerk when he said the word aloud.

"Your *knees*," he crowed.

"Yes," she screamed. "Yes, yes, yes. Now tell me how you got that scar."

"Okay," he relented. "I was ten years old and had just finished a marvelous book about an Indian fakir who walked on broken glass."

She sucked in her breath and moaned softly.

"I see you've already jumped ahead of me," he said, releasing her hands. "You're right. I decided if he could do it, so could I. And I did. Three steps worth. Crazy, huh?"

"What did your parents do to you?"

He grinned and shook his head. "Legs nearly tore my head off."

"Legs?"

"That's my pet name for my mom. The woman's got the best pair of legs I've ever seen—bar none."

"That's wonderful at any age but she must be . . . what? At least fifty-four? Fifty-five?"

"She's never admitted to any age. If anyone has the guts to point out to her that she has a thirty-four-year-old son, she just muddies the waters. I've heard her claim she found me on her doorstep, and she also says she was a child bride. Married at ten."

"So what did she do to you?"

"Actually it was what she said. 'Jeffrey, darling, if you ever pull a damn fool stunt like that again, I promise to put seven lumps on your empty little head.' " His falsetto imitation was priceless, Ann mused.

Ann told him he probably deserved worse. "I'll bet your dad really straightened you out, huh?"

Jeffrey's bittersweet smile and suddenly shadowed eyes revealed past sorrow. "No, he didn't do much about it. Mom was the disciplinarian in the family, I guess. Dad was a laid-back sort of guy. Nothing much fazed him. In the walking-on-glass episode, I think he gave me a little lecture about foolish behavior, cautioning me about trying it with hot coals."

He chuckled. "I distinctly remember his instructions, should I try the ultimate walk. If I were successful, I was to come to him at once; if I wasn't, I should be sure I knew how to swim." He paused. "God, I miss him."

"Has he been gone long, Jeff?" she asked softly, smoothing a curl off his forehead.

"Almost five years. But sometimes, when I need him, it feels like forever." He swallowed hard. "He was my best friend, Annie. Nothing ever seemed to bother him. No matter what I did, what I tried, good, bad, or indifferent, he was always on my side, showing me the better way. He was an honorable man." Jeffrey gently kissed her, then lifted his head to gaze into her eyes. "Dad would have liked you," he whispered. "I think you'd remind him a lot of my mother."

"How's that?" she asked, spellbound by his hypnotic gaze.

"Though she's always been totally feminine, she's one of the most gutsy ladies around. Street-smart, intelligent, and a powerhouse when it comes to getting things done."

"Sounds like my kinda woman," Ann said. "Does she live with you at Mountainview?"

Oh, damn, now you've done it, genius, Jeffrey berated himself. Be careful. "No," he said, kissing her again to distract her. "My mother lives wherever the mood takes her. Presently she makes her home on Mars. Or is it Jupiter? I forget." He trailed kisses to her ear, then sucked gently on her lobe.

"You're talking crazy."

"Then I'll stop talking. Haven't you some hair-raising childhood experience to share?"

She circled his neck with her arms and smiled.

"How about a little girl who took a dumb dare to sit on the center line of Highway 61 for an hour one Friday after school?"

Jeffrey gasped and cradled her in his arms. "And you lived to tell about it? Oh, Annie, you could have been killed."

"Like you, I was ten years old. And immortal. Anyway, it wasn't so bad until the trucks came."

"I'm almost afraid to ask."

"I think you've already guessed. The really scary times were when two trucks going in opposite directions passed at the same time." She shuddered at the memory. "The vacuum, or whatever was created, tried to suck me under the wheels."

"Poor baby. I'll bet you were glad when that hour was up."

She laughed. "Actually I lasted only forty-five minutes, which didn't look good on my dare record, but there wasn't a thing I could do about it."

"Somebody stopped you?"

"Boy, did he! My father's rig was the fourth truck that passed me going into town. He almost jackknifed slamming on his brakes. When he was finished with me, I'd promised never to sit in the middle of any highway for the rest of my natural life." She laughed again and rolled her eyes. "To tell you the truth, I couldn't sit *anywhere* for almost a week. You see, my *dad* was the disciplinarian at our house. Mom was the relaxed one in the family, though she often said they'd have to lock her away if she'd had more children than me."

"Only child?"

Ann nodded.

"Me too. Looks like we have at least one thing in common."

"We have the same crazy sense of humor," she said, "and we flirt with danger."

He gazed into her eyes, feeling himself falling. "We have at least two more things in common."

Ann waited.

"We both like to look at clouds."

"That's true," she said softly.

"And we both like to kiss . . . each other." He brushed a strand of hair off her rosy cheek. "And now that we're sharing our secrets, let's solve the last little mystery between us, shall we?"

Ann knew he was referring to how she knew about his scar, but couldn't suppress her guilty feeling about being her boss's official spy. Jeffrey had to rebuke himself as well. He'd be glad when this undercover work was finished and he could get everything out in the open with Ann.

"Whatever do you mean?" she asked, batting her eyes.

"I think I've figured out how you knew about the scar on the bottom of my heel."

"Oh, so now you're a private investigator, are you?"

He grimaced inwardly. She had no idea how right she was.

"You came into my room that first morning while I was fast asleep."

"I did not." She wiggled self-consciously but forced herself to relax again when Jeffrey grinned in obvious pleasure.

"Sure you did," he said. "You replaced my used drinking glass and hung the Do Not Disturb sign on the outside knob. *And* you spied on me while I was sleeping." He swiftly rolled onto his back, bringing Ann with him.

The change of position muddled Ann's denial. "I didn't mean to spy."

"Ah-ha!" He held her tight, adjusting her body on his.

"You didn't answer when I knocked . . . *hard.*" She tried to wedge her hands between their bodies to lift herself away from him.

"I was obviously sleeping," he said. He pulled her hands aside and smoothed back her silken hair.

"I thought you were dead."

"How did you find out I wasn't?" He toyed with the clasp of her bikini top.

"You scared the wits out of me by groaning, throwing the—I mean, turning over and snoring loud enough to wake the dead, that's how." She wiggled again, then stopped when he inhaled sharply.

"What else did you see beside my bare foot?" he asked. He separated his thighs and eased her down between them.

"Nothing," she said on a sigh, feeling her hips arch of their own volition.

"Not even when I threw off the covers?" He skimmed both hands down her smooth back and caressed her derriere, molding her body tightly against his.

She bit her lower lip and shut her eyes, tight.

He slid his hand along her hip, heading toward her knee. "Did I roll over on my back or my stomach?"

"Stomach," she blurted out before he could grab her kneecap.

"Well, that's something anyway. I hate to put on a show when I'm not even conscious," he said, laughing gruffly. "Did you like what you saw, Annie?"

His hands continued their sensual play. She could feel her body responding to his touch. She had to regroup and save the remnants of her tattered pride, she told herself.

"Well, I'll tell you, Jeff," she said lightly, even as her body seemed to be melting into his arms. "If you've seen one set of bare buns, you've seen them all."

"Stick out your tongue."

"Why?"

"Just do it," he ordered her. "Ah, just as I thought. Black."

"What does that mean?"

"Didn't you know your tongue turns black when you lie?"

"Circumstantial evidence."

"Your circumstantial snooping puts you one up on me."

"I can't stand a guy who insists on being equal."

"Nothing's equal about this. I had a definite handicap that morning."

"Yeah," she said, laughing even as Jeffrey rolled her onto her back. "You were unconscious."

He effectively stopped her laughter by dazzling her senses with a sizzling kiss. "I intend to be awake next time you come into my bedroom."

"Don't hold your breath."

"I won't, love," he whispered. His mouth grazed

hers. "Though I might hyperventilate." He kissed her deeply, his entire body moving against hers. His chest rubbed across her taut nipples, exciting them more with each brushing stroke, while his hips gently nudged hers until she parted her legs. He nestled against her, and she arched her back, moaning softly as she wrapped her arms tighter around his shoulders.

"I care for you, Annie," he murmured, caressing her face with tender kisses. "I care for you very much."

She sighed, longing to shed her mantle of guilt. Jeffrey cared for her. She cared for him. But she also had a promise she had to keep. What was she going to do? she wondered. She felt like a hypocrite, lying here in his warm embrace. Should she make a clean breast of it? Did she dare risk losing him when she explained? A shudder of fear rushed toward her heart. No, she thought, she couldn't tell him. Not now. Perhaps, never. Oh, it was all too complicated.

"Annie?" he said in a soft voice. "Where did you go, love?"

"Not far, Jeff. And now I'm back." She lifted her face for his kiss. "I'm right here."

When he kissed her again, Ann's heart took wing. Was she falling in love with him? she wondered. She knew she'd never felt like this before about any other man. And all these years she'd laughed when girlfriends who'd fallen in love claimed they heard music when their men kissed them! Why, she could hear a celestial chorus at this very moment. And she rejoiced in the sound.

Jeffrey's heart sang when Ann responded to his kiss. He was embracing a woman who, to him, was sunlight and bluebells and waterfalls and nectar. How could this be? he wondered. A moment ago they'd been wrestling like two children. Then, in a twinkling of an eye . . . no, in the space of one tender kiss, his world had taken on a rosy glow, a warmth beyond the season. My Lord, he thought. Was he falling in love with Annie?

Four

After Ann and Jeffrey finished a light supper at the Mosey Inn, they strolled arm in arm out to the screened porch overlooking the river. They sat on an old-fashioned white metal glider and watched the sun dip behind the horseshoe curve of the meandering stream, which turned crimson, then pink, then silver with the fading light.

Ann settled into the cradle of Jeffrey's arms, listening to the overture of the symphonic night sounds. Crickets chirped from their hiding places in the long grasses by the bank, a locust's song drifted from the woods, and in the distance a whippoorwill called its sweet refrain. She sighed, savoring the beauty of a near perfect day.

Jeffrey closed his eyes, amazed that the sounds he heard were so like those of his mountains. He smiled, realizing this night he could forgo the additional sound of the mosquitoes that usually whined in his ears when he was out in the wild. But where were the owls? he wondered, then smiled again and slid down in the cushions when he heard that faraway familiar call. All in all, he decided, it had been a day to remember.

"You have to admit we had a good day," Ann murmured, resting her head against his arm.

"Now, that's a fact." He gently stroked her hand. "I'm glad we spent it together. I think we could safely say we're friends now. What do you think?"

"I'd have to agree with you. We got to know each other better."

He laughed softly. "But I have to warn you, Annie. If you ever use any of my secrets against me, I'll get even with you."

"What?" she said, gasping and giggling simultaneously. "I can't believe you'd use violence."

"Naw," he said. "I'd kiss you till you screamed for mercy."

"That's a fate worse than death. Your threat might force me to inform on you. I daresay your mother could still take care of you."

"Legs?" he said, shaking his head. "That woman would probably take out a full-page ad in *The New York Times* if she ever found out I'd kissed a woman that much."

Ann turned to look at him, her eyes questioning. "I'm afraid I don't follow you."

"Well, it's like this," he said, lifting her hand to his lips to nibble her fingertips. "My mother wants me to get married. She says I've lived the wild life long enough. It's time to settle down."

"And what do you think?"

"I think—" He paused to ease her closer to him. "I think I'd make her the happiest woman in the world if I did. Trouble is, there's a hitch."

"A hitch?"

"Yes, I'd have to find the right woman first. It wouldn't do any good to marry if my wife refused to share my home."

"But if she loved you . . ."

He turned to Ann and saw concern in her eyes. "Would you leave everything and follow the man you loved?"

She broke from his penetrating gaze and began to toy with his hand. "He'd have to be a pretty special fellow to make me change my mind."

"And if he were?"

"I'd go . . . I think."

"Lady, you really know how to hedge your bets. Couldn't you just go for broke? Take a real risk?"

Ann thought the conversation had gone about as far as she was willing to let it. "I risked the day with you, didn't I?" she asked, giving his fingers a little squeeze. "Now, that's what I call risky."

"Yeah," he said, trailing a finger across her palm and sending spirals of delight shimmering up her arm and down her side. "Just you and me . . . and your CB, right?"

"Right." She tried to ease her hand from his grip, but he wouldn't release her. "Say, what do you do at night in your mountains when you meet up with a wolf?"

"They're scared of humans," he said, threading

his fingers with hers. "Unless they're starving." He gave her a little hug. "Have you had some trouble with wolves lately?"

"Nothing I couldn't handle, but I've been stalked by one or two in my day."

He leaned down and nuzzled the sensitive area behind her ear, drawing circles with the tip of his tongue, then blowing hot breath over the moist skin. "In Chicago?"

"Mostly."

"How about here?"

"So far there's been only you," she said pointedly. "I haven't been here very long."

"Suppose I told you I didn't want that to happen to you anymore?"

"You want me to stop seeing you?"

"No, dimwit," he scolded lovingly. "I'd like to be the only wolf . . . Damn, now you've got me saying it. Let me start again. I'd like to be the only man in your life."

"That's silly, Jeffrey. You'll be leaving any day now."

"Can't you indulge me while I'm here?"

"I suppose I could. But it doesn't make any sense. I'd be monopolizing your free time and perhaps you'd miss the woman of your dreams, not to mention your business appointments. Besides," she added, "what would your mother say to that? And another thing . . . we know so little about each other. Wouldn't you be bored hearing about my tame life, especially after you've been living on the wild side?"

"In answer to your questions: Don't worry about it . . . she doesn't know . . . and I'm fascinated. I love talking to you, Annie. So let's get started. Tell me one thing you hated in school."

"My secretarial courses," she answered, folding her arms across her chest. "I hated them so much I almost flunked. I never did master shorthand, but I learned to take dictation straight to the typewriter. I used to be a whiz at it before I went into the hotel business. What about you?"

"No question about it." He easily pried one of her hands free and clasped it firmly. "Macroeconomics. It almost stopped me from graduating from college. I had to take it more than once—don't ask me how many times—and I'm sure my last teacher finally took pity on me and gave me a mercy grade. I never could understand what was so all-fired important in that course. It didn't contain a thing I needed to run a business."

"Did you sweet-talk her?"

"Who?"

"Don't play dumb. Your teacher."

"You're assuming my teacher was a woman."

"Well, was she?"

"I never quite made up my mind about that."

"Jeffrey Madison, you are impossible!"

"That's what she used to say. Or was it he?"

He dodged the pillow Ann flung at him and gathered her in his arms. Her protest was muffled by a kiss so splendid she decided it would have made the dean's list in any college in the world. Before she drifted completely away with her feelings, she upgraded her opinion. Jeffrey could teach the definitive course. My, my, my, but that man could kiss!

When the embrace ended, they both were breathing heavily.

"Now then, what do you love?" Jeffrey asked.

Ann had to draw in a deep controlling breath before she answered. "The hotel business."

"Oh."

"Surely . . ." She turned to search his shadowed eyes. "Jeffrey, surely you didn't think I would say . . .?" Ann definitely did not believe in love at first sight.

"We do do it rather well, I think," he said.

It took her a moment to figure out what he meant. "Oh, you mean kiss."

"Of course I mean kiss. Heck, Annie, we haven't done anything else . . . yet."

She chose to ignore that last word. "I suppose kissing you is nice. Yes," she said, nodding. "I think I could say I like kissing you. But love? Uh-uh. That's too strong a word. I don't use it lightly. Ever. So many people say they *love* spaghetti. They *love* the Sunday comics. They *love* to say love."

"But you say you *love* the hotel business," he challenged her. "You're contradicting yourself."

"No, I'm not. I most certainly do *love* the hotel business. There's absolutely nothing like it. The biggest thrill for me is the behind-the-scenes hustle in order to make each guest feel special. If you'd worked in this field as long as I, you might love it too."

Jeffrey's heart sank when he saw how animated she was talking about the challenge of running a hotel, an occupation he thoroughly understood and wouldn't follow on a bet. He'd had his fill of it when he was growing up.

"Don't you like to travel?" he asked. "To see new places, meet new people?"

Her lighthearted laughter deflated his spirits even more. "I don't have to go out to discover the world," she said. "It comes to my door. Or at least to the hotel's door. No." She shook her head. "I think I'd die a little if I couldn't stay in this business. This is where I belong, Jeffrey. It's in my blood now."

That was the last thing he wanted to hear. "Hotels are usually located in cities," he grumbled. "I can't breathe in cities. Not for long, anyway."

He picked up a silken strand of her hair and feathered the curling tip. His sweet breath washed over Ann's throat and chin, and she licked her lips, trying to savor the taste of him. Did he know how it affected her when he played with her hair?

"That's the main reason why I built my offices on top of a mountain," he added.

He blew again, and Ann had to bite the inside of her cheek to suppress a little sigh.

"Up there," he went on, "I can experience nature constantly."

He twined the lock of hair around his fingers, occasionally grazing her neck in the most provocative and frustrating way. Ann knotted her hands in her lap and was unable to stop the small mewing sound that slipped from her parted lips.

Suddenly suspicious, she turned her head to look into Jeffrey's eyes. Nothing was there but a faraway preoccupied look. She watched him watch the wavy hair wind seductively around his fingers, and finally decided she could bet her pension that he was absolutely innocent of any underhanded motive. But if he didn't stop, she'd show him a little something about experiencing *her* nature.

"Living there is really wonderful," he whispered. "I can leave anytime I want, walk out the back door, and head for the trails. It's pretty heady stuff."

He brushed a stray tendril away from her face, and she captured his hand. Nature Boy didn't have any idea what he'd been doing to her emotions, she thought. Talk about heady stuff! What would she feel like if he put his mind to it?

"I think we'd better head back now, Jeff. Mr. and Mrs. Mosey like to close up by ten."

He looked at her speculatively, as if puzzled by her non sequitur, then nodded in agreement.

Back at the deserted shopping mall, Ann suggested they make plans for the next day. She wasn't sure which was making her feel more guilty: spying on Jeffrey for Vanessa, or taking advantage of Vanessa's waiving the rule about no fraternizing between employees and guests to spend more time with Jeffrey.

"How about a game of golf?" she asked. "Do you play?" The coy question left a bad taste in her mouth.

"Only for business, usually," he replied. "The best deals are often made on the course."

She could have gone all night without hearing that sort of an answer, she thought. Why couldn't he be just an ordinary fellow, free of suspicion? But his words caused her to put up her guard again. Was he recruiting from another company in the area?

Or was he headhunting within the hotel ranks? Lord, she wished she knew.

She waited with him until the taxi he'd called arrived. They decided to meet at the mall again at eight o'clock the next morning so they could get an early start.

"Don't be late, Annie," he whispered, feathering a sweet warm kiss across her lips.

"I won't," she promised, then pulled him back for another kiss. "Sleep well."

Chuckling, he opened his door and got out, then walked around to her side and leaned down to the opened window.

"Annie, you never want to end one of our evenings by teasing me," he advised, his long fingers capturing her neck in a careful vise. "I tend to tease right back."

He commenced to kiss her senseless which, Ann had to admit, was just down the road from breathless and excited. She moaned as his insistent tongue plunged repeatedly between her parted lips, and wondered if the cab driver could hear her. But there wasn't a thing she could do about it. Jeffrey's strong hand kept her head imprisoned under his wild attack. As if she'd be fool enough to want to escape!

When he released her, she was gasping. "Jeffrey Madison. That was wholly unfair. I was not teasing you."

"I wasn't teasing either." He smiled crookedly, then winked and blew her a kiss. " 'Night, love. I'll have the driver follow you back to make sure you get there safely."

• • • •

Though it was a gorgeous morning, Ann was not feeling chipper as she drove back to the shopping mall. In her mind she replayed her earlier meeting with Vanessa. It hadn't turned out exactly the way Ann had planned. After she'd made her report and her boss had applauded her resourcefulness, Ann had tried to withdraw from the assignment.

"I'd rather not do this anymore, Mrs. Cummings. I'm beginning to like him."

Vanessa had instantly jumped up from her chair and begun her pacing. "Maybe our suspicions are wrong," she'd said. "But I need your help to find out. Oh, please, Ann. Don't back out now."

It had seemed so important, there was nothing else Ann could do. She agreed to continue her surveillance. Vanessa had then rushed her right out of the office, not giving Ann a chance for more discussion. She suspected the hurried dismissal had something to do with the phone call Vanessa had received and put on hold while Ann was there.

Jeffrey tossed his clubs into the trunk of his rented car, slammed the lid down, and glanced at his watch. "Damn," he muttered. "I'm going to be late."

The whole day had started off wrong, he thought as he sped down the hotel drive. First, he'd called his mother to report in. She'd put him on hold. Although it couldn't have been more than a minute or two, it had seemed as though he'd sat there listening to dead air for at least an hour. It was just that he was eager to be with Ann.

When his mother had come back on the line, he'd insisted on seeing her. In the flesh. He wanted to be assured she was feeling all right and wasn't pulling one of her tricks.

She had agreed to see him. "But you'll have to come after midnight, when the hotel is quiet," she'd added. "I don't want anyone seeing you come up here. Do you still have your key?"

It had taken him another five minutes to find the key and inform his mother that he'd see her after midnight as she directed.

"Her and her damn cloak-and-dagger intrigue," he grumbled as he passed another car. "I could have been there by now."

Finally he pulled into the mall and found a parking spot near Ann's Corvette. "Hi, Ann," he called. He took a deep breath and decided nothing else was going to upset him today. "Been waiting long?"

"Just a few minutes," she replied, pushing her large-framed sunglasses onto her head as she watched him get out of his car. "You look like you're ready for the links." Her gaze slid up and down his attractive frame. He was dressed in gray slacks and a red knit shirt. "Love your shirt."

He kissed her hello, then scrutinized her own outfit. She was a knockout in a short golf dress and matching headband. "I followed a hunch this morning. I was betting you'd wear red too." He smiled as he recalled the red bathing suit she'd worn the day before. "You do look good in red."

She grinned. "Thanks. Are you ready to go?"

They decided to take his car, since its large trunk

could easily accommodate both sets of clubs. At the golf course they had to wait before they could tee up at the first hole, but it was only a brief wait.

Much to Jeffrey's surprise, Ann really gave him a run for his money. It was partly his fault, he silently admitted while he tried to concentrate on his last shot. During the first five holes he'd laid back, enjoying the sunshine and fresh air, and, quite honestly, never expected any real competition from his partner. By the seventh hole she'd had him sweating, and by the eighth they were tied for par. The lead went back and forth until they were again tied at the eighteenth hole. He got a birdie, but Ann had to swing from the edge of the green.

He made his putt without any trouble, but vowed never to underestimate Ann again. She was a fine player. When she needed two strokes to make her shot, he was truly sorry.

"You played a fine game, Annie," he said, draping his arm over her shoulders. "I thought for sure you'd make that shot from the back of the cup. Tough break."

"Yeah, well, we couldn't both win," she said stoically.

They hefted their golf bags and walked in silence for several yards. Then Jeffrey came to a halt and turned Ann to face him. She lifted her gaze to meet his, and he peered searchingly into her eyes.

"What is it?" she asked, concern shadowing her face.

"Annie . . ." he began. "Annie, if I thought for a minute that you'd thrown the game, I'd . . . I'd be very upset with you."

"Jeffrey, that's the most ridiculous idea I've ever heard," she said, staring at him incredulously. "Can you really picture me, of all people, *arranging* things so the big wonderful man can win the game? Really, Jeff, I'm surprised you'd even entertain such a thought. Besides, I had five dollars riding on that game, and I was taught never to throw away money."

He smiled, and Ann thought it was the nicest smile she'd ever seen. He seemed quite pleased about the whole thing.

"I don't want your money, Annie."

"You may not want it, Mr. Madison, but you *will* take it. I always pay up on my bets."

"You're no welsher, I know that. I'm just saying I wish you'd forget about it." He took her hand and smiled down at her serious features. "I'll bet you would have told me the same thing."

"Probably," she said, "but that's not my style."

"Nor mine, Annie."

She laughed. "Well, Mr. Madison, it seems we're having a Mexican standoff."

"Let me think about it," he said.

They continued their walk toward the clubhouse in silence.

Ann was feeling great as she relived the morning. A good game, played fairly. A friendly argument. A few laughs. Just like a regular couple, she thought. Then she wondered where that idea had come from, giving her head a little shake.

"Okay," Jeffrey finally said. "You buy lunch today."

"What? Oh, lunch. Now, where in the world are we going to get two lunches for five dollars?"

"I know just the place," he said, giving her a quick kiss. "I'll take you there after we shower and change."

Dressed in faded jeans and comfortable knit shirts, Ann and Jeffrey sat near the river at an umbrella table in the city park, dining on chili dogs with everything on them and old-fashioned root beer in iced mugs. Later, walking along First Street, they window-shopped and munched on chocolate chip cookies. By five o'clock they were both so tired they didn't think they could walk another step.

"Refreshment time," Jeffrey announced, dragging Ann toward a restored pre-World War II ice cream parlor.

"I'm going to melt before we get there," she wailed.

"Come on, love," he said encouragingly. "Three more steps and you'll be in air-conditioning."

Once inside the cool shop, he led her to a little round table and two matching ice cream parlor chairs.

"Here, honey, sit down," he said. He eased her into one of the chairs, then slipped into the other one. "Now, what would you like to have?"

Ann allowed herself one silent moment of insanity, and thought, *You!* Then she shook her head and grinned. "One bathtub, filled to the brim with ice," she said, laughing.

Solemnly, Jeffrey gazed around the empty cheerful room. "Sorry but I don't think they have anything that large. I do see a big pitcher on the shelf behind the soda fountain. Would that do?"

"I suppose I could dip myself in it one limb at a time."

His gaze softened with concern. "You are hot, aren't you?"

Was she ever! she thought. Although Jeffrey had been affectionate today, most of his caresses had been casual—taking her hand as they walked, dropping brief kisses on her cheek or forehead. Rather than diminishing her sensual awareness of him, those light touches had heightened it, and she was feeling unbelievably aroused—and frustrated!

"I'm a little warm around the edges," she said, "but I'll be all right in a minute."

"Hi, neighbors. I'm Wally." The red-haired soda jerk wore a white cap balanced at a jaunty angle. He grinned and placed two frosty glasses of ice water on the table, then handed them each a menu. "I'll be back in a flash to take your order."

Ann leaned forward to whisper to Jeffrey, and he leaned forward to listen. "Are you sure we didn't step back in time when we came in here?" she asked.

"I wouldn't be surprised if he started to strut and talk about the 'bee's knees,' " Jeffrey said, chuckling.

They straightened in their chairs when the smiling waiter returned.

"Well, what'll it be, folks?" he asked, pencil poised above his order pad. "We got anything your little hearts desire." He grinned from ear to ear. "That is, anything in ice cream treats."

Jeffrey glanced at the menu and quickly made his choice. "I'll have a banana split."

"We got a special on the deluxe today," Wally said. "You interested?"

Jeffrey gazed for a moment at Ann, who was studying her menu, and thought that he was more interested than Wally would ever know. "Why not?" he said. "Be creative."

"And you, miss?"

"Would you mind telling me what goes into a deluxe banana split?" she asked.

Wally gave her another toothy grin. "I was hopin' you'd ask. This is gonna knock your socks off. Ready?"

Ann closed her menu and gave him her full attention. "Ready."

"You get three scoops of 'cream, one flavor or mixed, in chocolate, strawberry, or vanilla. You picks. The toppings are luscious: hot fudge, butterscotch, and 'berry. Then it's trimmed with whipped cream, chopped nuts, and a cherry."

Ann and Jeffrey applauded enthusiastically.

"Bravo, Wally," Ann said. "That was wonderful. You ought to be on the stage."

"Ain't it the cat's pajamas?" he said. "I worked up the routine last week. Sure has increased business."

Jeffrey looked around the empty room.

Wally caught the unspoken message. "Hey, folks, you're here, ain't cha?"

"We certainly are, Wally," Ann said, laughing. "I'll follow my friend's lead and ask you to create something special for me too."

"Holy cow," he exclaimed. "Two 'Wally Specials' in one day. You ain't gonna believe this, folks." He snapped shut his order book and two-stepped back to the counter.

"I'm sure we've entered the twilight zone," Ann said.

Jeffrey's only reply was to lean forward and hum the first few bars of the program's theme song. Then he glanced over his shoulder at the young man, who was, indeed, strutting his stuff. "Annie," he whispered, "get a gander at that performance."

She made a face at his choice of words, then turned to watch Wally. He was extraordinary, she thought. He didn't just scoop the ice cream into the clear glass dishes. He actually threw the scoops up into the air in a large arc, behind his back and over his shoulder. After the toppings were ladled on and the whipped cream piled in billowing mounds, he sprinkled on the nuts, then tossed a cherry into the air and held the dish up so that the cherry landed in the middle with a gentle plop.

"You're a true aficionado of soda fountain art," Jeffrey said when Wally set the banana splits before him and Ann.

"And I ain't bad makin' banana splits either," he said. "Enjoy!"

"Mmmm, don't they look delicious?" Ann said. She lifted her spoon, ready to dig in. "Trade you my cherry for some of your nuts," she said, picking up her maraschino cherry by its stem.

Unfortunately, at the same moment Jeffrey was taking a long drink from his water glass. Upon hearing her words he spewed water into his napkin and coughed for a full minute. His choking so alarmed Ann that she sprang from her chair and began beating him on his back.

Now you can be sure you'll never, ever miss a single Loveswept title by enrolling in our special reader's home delivery service. A service that will bring all four new Loveswept romances published every month into your home—and deliver them to you before they appear in the bookstores!

Examine 4 Loveswept Novels for

15 days FREE!

(SEE OTHER SIDE FOR DETAILS)

"Jeffrey," she cried. "Are you all right, honey?"

Red-faced and almost unable to speak, he croaked, "Sure, Annie, I'm fine. A piece of ice slipped down my throat." He wheezed. "Lord, it felt as big as an iceberg."

"Well, just sit quietly for a minute and you'll feel better," she said, taking her seat again. "Do you?"

He lifted his bloodshot eyes questioningly.

She sighed patiently. "Want to trade?"

"Yes," he said soberly. "That is, if you're sure."

"Silly," she said, placing her cherry next to the one on top of his dish, then helping herself to a spoonful of chopped peanuts. "I wouldn't have offered if I weren't sure."

It was more than a few minutes before Jeffrey could eat his banana split.

Outside, the temperature had cooled with the setting sun, and they strolled hand in hand through the twilight to the car. Before they got in, Jeffrey leaned against the door, his legs spread wide, pulled Ann into his arms, and gave her one of the most adult kisses she'd ever experienced. When it ended, they stood for a few moments, body to body, just feeling, savoring the powerful attraction pulling them together. It pulsated between them like a live thing that had a mind all its own.

"I can't get enough of your kisses," Jeffrey said. "I want to hold you in my arms forever, kiss you endlessly, give you pleasure that never stops." He traced her full lips with a trembling finger. "Annie, I think I'm falling in love with you."

Were her ears deceiving her? she wondered. Had Jeffrey said he was falling in love with her, Ann Waverly of Weir, Kansas? Her eyes grew wide with surprise. Yes, he'd said it.

"I think I'm falling in love with you too," she whispered.

"Are you sure, honey?" he asked, trying to read the answer in her smoky eyes.

She shook her head slowly. "No, I'm not absolutely sure, but then, I've never felt this way before."

"The feeling's new to me too. I just know I want to be with you all the time."

"Do you think that's love?"

He chuckled, and the rumble from his chest vibrated straight into her heart. "If it's not, it sure must be a close relative," he said.

"Probably a kissin' cousin." Oh, listen to her, she thought. Now wasn't the time for joking. "Forget I said that." Embarrassed, she leaned her head against his chest. The heat from his strong body did nothing to cool her cheeks.

"Ann, darling," he said, lifting her chin to gaze into her eyes. "I want to make love to you. Very much." He slid his large hands down to her hips. "I want to do all those things I mentioned. I want to hold you in my arms, kiss you, give you pleasure." He punctuated each phrase with a heart-stopping kiss.

"I want that too, Jeff," she answered, trembling in his arms.

"I saw a little inn just around the corner. Let's have dinner there and stay for the night."

She smoothed a golden curl from his brow, and sadly shook her head. "I can't, Jeff. Not tonight. I work switchboard in the morning."

He leaned forward and touched his forehead to hers. "I forgot tomorrow was Monday. I hate to agree with you, but you're right. If we were together tonight, we'd be awake till morning."

"You think so?" she asked, intrigued.

"I *know* so." He sighed with resignation. "So we'll go to the inn, but only for dinner."

"Sounds as if we have something good to look forward to, huh?" She was trying desperately to lighten the mood, to make him smile . . . and forget that yawning ache between them.

"Ms. Waverly," he began, threading his fingers through her hair. "Love," he whispered. His breath bathed her lips with warmth. "When the time is right, we're going to share something so good, it will be unbelievably beautiful." He kissed her again, long and sweet and tender. "Annie, you can bet the farm on this one," he promised.

It was exactly midnight when Jeffrey walked into his mother's apartment. He spent ten minutes questioning her about her health. Although he was not completely satisfied with her answers, she made him stop.

"Jeffrey, darling, you're beginning to sound like a character on *Hill Street Blues.* Please, son. Stop grilling me."

Frustrated, he massaged the back of his neck and stared out the window at the sliver of new moon rising over the river. "Dammit, Mom, I care about you. How the hell can I make you understand how much I care?"

"By giving me enough credit to know what I can and cannot do," she said. "I told you once, son. I'm not interested in pedestal-sitting. It's a boring existence. Furthermore, any woman interested in being treated as an equal would say the same. When are you going to realize that?"

"Tell me about it," he muttered, remembering the run for his money Ann had given him on the golf course.

His mother watched him shrewdly. "Jeffrey Madison Cummings, if I didn't know better, I'd say you were falling in love." She walked over to him and put her hand on his shoulder, patting gently. "What is it, dear?"

Jeffrey wasn't sure he would have told his mother even if he'd known what had turned him into a snapping turtle. "I'm just beat, Legs. I think I'll turn in." He kissed her on the cheek. "Good night, Mom. I love you."

Later, when he lay in his darkened room, he couldn't sleep. He kept trying to find answers in the shadows. It wasn't like him to argue with his mother. To tease her, yes. But she was right. Tonight he'd sounded like some television cop grilling a suspect.

Dragging the sheet up over his hips, he rolled onto his side, searching his memory for a particular piece of advice from his father. What had he said that day up on Maribee Pass? Finally, after several minutes, the elusive conversation bubbled up into his conscious mind.

His father had advised Jeffrey on how to keep love once he was lucky enough to receive it. "Hold it close, but not too close. Protect it with your life, but let it have a life of its own.

"Above all else, never doubt love. I promise you, if you'll do these things for love, then love will bless you every day of your life."

Jeffrey wiped a tear from his cheek. He recalled asking his father how long he would have to wait for love.

"Maybe it will come to you tomorrow," he'd said, smiling. "Perhaps you'll have to wait for many years. But when it comes, son, you'll know it. I promise you, Jeff. You'll know it. Then you'll remember all I've told you today."

Jeffrey had always trusted his dad's advice, had consistently believed all his father had shared with him. But in this case he wasn't so sure. His father had promised he would remember the conversation when love came. Well, he'd remembered his father's advice, and yet he wasn't sure he was in love with Ann. Not absolutely iron-clad sure.

"Dammit, Dad," he whispered, crushing his pillow in his arms. "I need you. I need to talk to you."

Sleep—night's tempting mistress—eluded Jeffrey's capture for many hours.

Five

"Good morning, Mr. Madison. It's seven o'clock."

"What the . . .? I didn't order a wake-up call," he grumbled, squinting to see his watch. Then he heard a very small chuckle on the other end of the phone. "Annie, is that you?"

"Yes, sir."

Moaning softly, he fell back against his pillows. " 'Morning, love," he whispered, drawing out the words as he stretched. "I could get used to waking up to your voice every morning. Of course, I'd want the warm, gorgeous body that goes along with it too." He sighed disconsolately, hoping to make her squirm. "If you'd said yes last night, I'd be holding you in my arms right now. Oh, Annie, *I need you*."

The fervid conviction of his unexpected statement produced a sudden burst of heat inside Ann, which threatened to overload her emotional thermostat.

She tried not to sigh too loudly. Her supervisor was lurking somewhere behind her.

The man was certainly plain spoken, if not incendiary, she thought, trying to calm her galloping heart. It had taken only three words—*I need you*—to light her fire.

She cleared her throat. "Your complimentary coffee and newspaper will be at your door within fifteen minutes. Will that be convenient, sir?"

He heard the forced cordiality in her voice and smiled. She wasn't as unaffected as she was trying to make him believe. "I don't suppose you could deliver it personally?"

"No, sir. That's next week."

"You mean you might come to my door?"

"I might."

"I'm never dressed that early. I probably would answer the door wearing only a towel and shock your system, Annie-girl."

"Me, sir? No, sir." But she allowed a little giggle to mar her businesslike tone.

"Happens every day, does it?"

"Just about, sir."

She answered so casually, Jeffrey wasn't so sure she was kidding anymore. Stroking his beard-rough cheek, he tried a different tack. "You made me lose sleep last night, lady."

"No!" she gasped, not quite able to keep the laughter from her quavering voice.

"Probably have to take a nap this afternoon," he went on. "I owe you one, kid."

"Not true, sir."

"You mean . . . ?"

"'Fraid so, sir."

He didn't even try to suppress his triumphant laughter. "Can I see you after work? I'd like to take you to the Jade Room for dinner."

"I believe that can be arranged."

"Same place? Seven o'clock?"

"Yes, sir. Have a good day, Mr. Madison."

"It's gonna be a damn long one," he said. "I wish we could be together earlier, but you'll want a little time to rest before you get ready." He cleared his throat. "If I had my way, you'd be here with me right now."

This time her heartfelt sigh was clearly audible over the line. "I couldn't agree with you more. Thank you, sir."

After replacing the receiver in its cradle, Jeffrey rolled out of bed, slipped on his navy velour robe, and pulled open the beige brocade drapes covering the picture window. His suite was located on the wrong side of the hotel as far as he was concerned.

The view was strictly manmade. There was a symmetrically perfect concrete pond surrounded by sculptured shrubbery, flower beds, and manicured lawns. The artificial scene was an affront to the great outdoors, he thought, frowning. Beyond that there were only buildings, "nothing but bricks and mortar."

He wished for a high mountain trail shrouded in morning mist, the ground dusted with hoarfrost awaiting the new sunrise. In his imagination he stood at the crest of Murphy's Ridge, breathing in the cold crisp air, feeling cleansed in body and soul after a night spent under the stars. Whenever he gazed into the awakening valley, its virgin forest still blanketed in the smoky blue haze of dawn, he recognized his insignificance in the universe. His contribution to life would probably go unnoticed by most of the human race. He could accept that because he was satisfied with the goodness of what he did, whether it was capturing a criminal, rescuing a lost child, or working to save an endangered species.

Would Ann ever share a climb with him? he wondered. He smiled as he pictured her in his mind: khaki walking shorts, red plaid flannel shirt, sturdy hiking boots, a nylon pack on her back, her long shining hair in two thick braids. She'd probably enjoy vacationing in the mountains, he decided, since she seemed to appreciate and cherish the beauty of untouched land.

But try as he might, he couldn't imagine her permanently in a pastoral setting. She loved city living too much, and her life revolved around her career in the hotel business. Ann honestly believed the world came to her door. She thrived on the multitude of duties she was asked to perform in order to serve the public. The excitement, the challenges, the behind-the-scenes preparation all gave her a rush, a natural high.

For himself, he'd had his fill of that kind of life when he was growing up. Every day was a series of small and large crises—lost keys, broken televisions, kids locked in bathrooms, stopped-up toilets . . . usually caused by the kids locked in the bathrooms.

No, he wanted no part of the hotel business. He didn't know if he'd ever be able to convince his mother of that, but he really meant it. He was content with his company back home in Mountainview. He never wanted to live anywhere else.

He gazed out the window again, then examined the window casing. "Unbelievable!" he muttered. He couldn't open a window if he wanted to. He had to get away, he realized. It was a good thing he'd made arrangements to play golf with Charles today. Even this spacious suite was shrinking, trapping him. How did Ann stand it? he wondered, heading for the shower.

Downstairs in the employees' lounge, Ann put her feet up and smiled, recalling her conversation with Jeffrey. He was a lot of fun. But being with him was a little like riding a roller coaster. She never knew when he was going to turn serious.

She sipped her black coffee. The weekend had been very special. They'd had a good time. More than a good time! It had been downright delicious in some areas. Like when they kissed. Ann couldn't remember when she'd ever become so easily aroused by a simple kiss. Not simple, she qualified. Nothing about Jeffrey Madison was simple, she was discovering. He kissed and caressed like a mature man. But he also retained a sense of wonder, a little boy's delight in all things, large and small.

How many men would be content to lie on a blanket in the middle of a meadow, watching the ever-changing clouds? And how many men were secure enough in their maleness to brush a woman's hair just for the sheer joy of seeing it shine? Never mind the sensual pleasure he'd given to the woman. Not many men, Ann guessed, could do that without making some kind of wisecrack about gay hairdressers.

"And he thinks he's falling in love with me," she whispered dreamily. His hand had trembled on her lips when he'd said the words. Had it been the first time he'd ever spoken of love to a woman? she wondered. Surely, a man of his obvious experience would have known love before. But he'd agreed with her when she'd told him she didn't know how it should feel. The thought of loving someone, perhaps finding one's mate, was apparently new to them both. How wonderful! she thought, to be falling in love for the first time . . . together.

But even as she began to get carried away by the euphoria of love, reality brought her crashing back down to earth. She might be falling in love with a man who was working against the River Regency. What was he going to do today? she wondered. Would he go golfing again with one of the key employees of the hotel? And if he did, how would she be able to find out, stuck back in the switchboard room?

She sighed, then finished her coffee. She'd carefully quiz Jeffrey this evening, and perhaps be able to read between the lines. Then she'd make her final report to her boss and resign from the spy business.

But if Jeffrey were truly planning a raid of the hotel's key personnel, she'd never be able to forgive him. And where would that leave their relationship? "Up the creek without a paddle," she mumbled, getting up to refill her cup.

She tried to examine her relationship with Jeffrey. She admitted that she had strong feelings for him. Ha! she chided herself. Be honest. You think you're falling in love with the man. Beside the possibility of his being an executive raider—which had yet to be proven, she was quick to point out—what was there not to like? He was handsome, bright, playful, caring, able to apologize when it was necessary, and humble in victory.

She grinned when she recalled how hard that last virtue had been for him after the golf game. The little boy in him had wanted to whoop and dance a jig!

Best of all, the chemistry between them didn't feel forced. It felt natural. Like eating. Or breathing. The most natural thing in the world. Which was why she hadn't wanted to leave him last night. "What am I going to do?" she muttered.

"About what?"

She spun around so quickly, she almost knocked her coffee cup off the table. "Jeffrey, how did you get in here? This room is off-limits to guests."

"Piece of cake, Annie." He took her into his arms and kissed her long and hard before she had a chance to refuse him.

She melted against him, softly moaning in surrender. He tightened his hold on her, and his tongue rubbed languidly over her lips, her tongue. His hands smoothed down her back until he cupped her rounded bottom and held her firmly against his aroused body.

Ann's fingers crept over his broad shoulders to

play in his thick hair. She arched her hips, rubbing against him until he groaned with frustration.

"Lord, Annie, I can't stand to be away from you for a minute," he said. His words shot straight to her heart.

When she pulled on his head, trying to bring his mouth back to her deserted lips, Jeffrey knew he was going to have to put the brakes on his desires. If Ann's reaction to his sudden appearance was any indication, she wasn't going to help him at all. He doubted she knew where she was at the moment.

"Run away with me, love," he whispered. "To the land of dreams come true. I'll worship at your feet . . . not to mention the rest of your gorgeous body." He waggled his brows like Groucho Marx.

In a mental fog, Ann stared at Jeffrey. "I'm on my coffee break," she said inconsequentially.

"Stranger things have happened on coffee breaks," he teased, giving her another Groucho look.

"Oh!" she gasped, finally able to pull herself back to reality. She was not, however, strong enough to withdraw from Jeffrey's embrace. "Darn it," she said. "You caught me off guard." She smoothed her hair back, not yet able to meet his steady gaze.

"Admit it," he said. "I turn you on."

She smiled winsomely. "You do." Then her smile became sensual. "But I'll bet everything I've got that I affect you in the same way."

"I won't deny it," he said. "That's what I've been trying to show you, Annie." He locked his hands behind her back and pulled her closer, closer. "I *want* everything you've got to give."

"Will you stop?" she squeaked, feeling herself beginning to drown in his smoldering blue eyes.

"Probably not," he said, grinning. "So . . . what are you going to do about it?"

Oh, Lordy, she thought. She was going to have to do some fast talking. How did she always get herself into such crazy predicaments? "The question is," she said, "how did you get in here? And why?"

"That's two questions," he pointed out. "I got in here on my own size elevens. And"—he raised one brow and leaned closer—"have you forgotten the why so quickly, my dear?" His mouth captured hers in a torrid kiss of breathtaking proportions. "That's why, Annie," he murmured, rubbing noses with her and then kissing her forehead.

Completely disoriented, she kissed him back. "But you're not supposed to be here."

"I know, love, but I also knew I'd never make it through the day without holding you, kissing you."

"That's nice," she said dreamily. She kissed him again, adoring the taste of him. "But you're not supposed to be here."

He led her back to the couch and sat her down. Smiling whimsically, he bent to give her one last kiss. It was a very long kiss, primarily because Ann continued to surge forward every time Jeffrey eased away.

"I'm leaving now, love," he finally said.

She took a handful of his shirt and pulled him back. "Okay." She kissed him again.

Coming up for air, Jeffrey took a deep breath and tried again. "I'm out of here now, Annie."

She nodded and nuzzled his neck.

Patiently unfolding her slender fingers from his shirt, he fought to catch his breath as well as his balance. "Annie love, I'll see you tonight."

And he was gone.

Afterward, Ann figured she had probably sat there for several minutes before she finally snapped out of her stupor. That man was like quicksilver, she thought dazedly. Now you see him, now you don't. And she was excited by every sparkling inch of him— whether he was in person or only in her mind.

But was there a chance for a lasting relationship with Jeffrey Madison, the nature boy? she asked herself. He'd certainly enjoyed their day in the country. For that matter, so had she. But she knew he loved the country enough to live there. Didn't he rave about the pure air and uncluttered beauty on his mountaintop? And the peace and quiet?

She thought it sounded nice, too, but what if she moved there? Assuming Jeffrey asked her, of course. Even though it was a hypothetical question, she knew the answer—she'd be crazy inside of a week without the excitement and challenge of her career.

Ann could stand only so much tranquillity before she had to break loose and find a little action. It was like an itch. Sometimes she could handle it, but when she couldn't stand it anymore, she simply had to scratch.

She wouldn't change, even if she could, she thought, folding her arms across her chest. There wasn't a thing wrong with the way she liked to live. It was just different from Jeffrey's way. He was the nature boy and she was the city chick. And she didn't see where either of them would ever be able to compromise.

But she wasn't going to worry about it, she decided, shrugging. There were fifty-fifty odds on every question she faced concerning Jeffrey. Either he was an executive raider, or he wasn't. Either they'd make love, or they wouldn't. If they both wanted a lasting relationship, they'd compromise. Or they'd part.

Ann drew in a tremulous breath at that last alternative. At the moment she couldn't think of one avenue leading toward a possible compromise. Would she and Jeffrey have to part and go their separate ways?

In her room that evening Ann changed her clothes five times before she was satisfied with her outfit. Her first choice, a ruffled white sundress, was too frivolous. After going through the color spectrum—a peach skirt and blouse, a sleeveless red jumpsuit, a tailored cotton dress in royal blue—she arrived at the other extreme.

The black silk dress had long sleeves, and was slinky and sophisticated. Although it covered her from the neck to below her knees, it clung lovingly to her, revealing every tantalizing curve of her firm high breasts, her softly rounded hips, her shapely thighs.

She slipped on black stockings and stepped into spike-heeled ankle-strap shoes. Her hair was swept up in a smooth chignon. She applied her makeup so that her eyes appeared wide and smoky, even a little wild. Her red lipstick and fingernail polish accentuated that image. Next she put on a black velvet choker with a large white silk camellia fastened at the side.

The final touch was a generous anointing of all her pulse points with the most expensive, exotic perfume she owned. Just knowing she was wearing the sultry fragrance made her feel sinfully decadent.

She gazed into her mirror. Terrific! She looked again and frowned. Not terrific. Something wasn't quite right. She studied her image, then smiled. With her comb she eased short tendrils of hair from her perfect hairdo. She smiled. The little wisps of dark curls softened her features, accented her femininity.

She picked up her black envelope purse and headed for the door, but the phone delayed her departure.

"Ann?" Vanessa Cummings said when Ann answered the phone. "I just thought I'd call to see if anything's developing in our spy case. Are you keeping tabs on our mystery man?"

"Yes, I am." But not for long, boss, she added silently.

"Any progress?"

Ann almost laughed at the loaded question. If she didn't know better, she'd think she was being set up. Now, that was a thought! Here she was, questioning her own boss's motives. The poor woman had come from a sick bed to face a possible attempt to dismantle her managerial staff. Ann decided she was becoming paranoid over the issue of Jeffrey

Madison's culpability, and felt very ashamed of herself. She knew her boss was above suspicion.

"I'm not sure what he did today," she said, "but I'm going to have dinner with him this evening. I hope I'll have more to tell you in the morning."

'Now don't overtax yourself, Ann. I won't have you working day and night just so we can catch this man in the act."

This conversation was going to overtax her brain, Ann thought, if she didn't stop finding double entendres in every one of her boss's innocuous statements.

"Don't worry about me," she said, trying to sound light and cheerful. "I can handle Jeffrey Madison."

"I never doubted it, dear. I hope you enjoy your evening. I'll talk to you tomorrow."

Ann hung up and hurried downstairs to her car. As she sped out of the parking lot she checked her watch. She was going to be very late.

Several miles down the road Jeffrey stood inside the phone booth to the post office, talking to his mother.

"I'm checking in, Mom," he said. "How was your day? I hope you're not working too hard."

"Consider yourself checked, love," she said, laughing. "My day has gone better than I could have hoped. And I'm not working any harder than I have for the last thirty-five years."

"I don't suppose it'll do a bit of good for me to ask you to take it easier."

"If I give you my programmed answer, I'll begin to sound like a broken record, darling. Of course, if you want to hear it again . . ."

"Naw, that's okay."

"Are you sure?" she teased. "I'll rest when you give me my— "

"Mom, please. Spare me."

"Would you like to have dinner with me, son? I'll have the cook make your favorites."

"Gee, Mom, I'd like nothing better, but . . . ah . . . ah—"

"Jeffrey, you're going to be thirty-five years old in a few months," she interrupted. "How old do you suppose you'll be before you can tell me straight out that you've got a heavy date?"

"What makes you think it's heavy?" he asked, chuckling.

"You're your father's son. Could you have any other kind?"

"Touché, Legs." If every man had a mother like his, Jeffrey thought, the world would be a better place.

"Anyone I know?" she asked.

"I doubt if you've ever met this woman, Mom," he answered, careful not to lie. His mother had already told him she was far too busy to interview lower-level personnel.

"Is she nice?"

"Yes, she is."

"*How* nice, Jeffrey?"

"Very nice, Mom."

"Nice enough to bring home to meet your mother?"

"I don't know yet," he hedged, easily reading between the lines. "We're just getting acquainted. I'm taking her to dinner tonight."

"Now, son, I hope you'll be careful. Your father would never forgive me if I let you fall into the arms of some wily, unscrupulous female. You're such a handsome, intelligent, darling boy. Not to mention your wealth and considerable real estate holdings and your—"

Jeffrey's laughter finally stopped his mother's litany of his finer qualities. He thought it was hilarious how she always glossed over or completely ignored his faults. It also never failed to delight him, and to make him feel ten feet tall. Although he had never discussed it with his father, he suspected his mother had made him feel the same way. She never stopped telling her husband how wonderful she thought he was.

Did every wife and mother do that for her husband and children? Jeffrey wondered. It wasn't such a bad idea. If no one else in the world appreciated a woman's family, she'd do it herself, unselfishly, unendingly.

"Now, Legs," he said, "I don't want you to worry about me. I can handle a-any woman. Except you."

"I never doubted it, darling."

Her instant about-face took him by surprise. "Mom?"

"I hope you enjoy your evening with . . . whoever she is," she said, laughing mysteriously. "I'll talk to you tomorrow. Good night, Jeffrey."

"'Night, Mom."

He shook his head as he hung up the phone. He

didn't think he'd ever fully understand his mother. Or any woman, for that matter. But he'd always follow his father's advice: Just love them. Don't try too hard to understand them.

Ten minutes later a police car roared into the parking lot, red lights flashing, siren blaring, and screeched to a halt in front of the post office. Directly behind it was a red Classic Corvette. It whipped around the police car and stopped in the parking space next to Jeffrey's rented black Lincoln.

Before he could say a word or make a move, Ann emerged from her car—a bewitching vision—and dazzled him with a brilliant smile.

"Hi," she said breathlessly. "I'm sorry I'm late."

"Are you all right?" he asked, not yet believing his eyes. He was blinded by her beauty as well as being distracted by the lights still blinking on the roof of the police car. At least they'd turned off the siren.

"I'm just fine," she said. She locked her car and dropped the keys into her purse, then turned to the two officers standing by their car. "Thanks, fellas. That was a wild ride."

"Anytime, Ann," one called, giving her a laid-back salute.

"Did we make it in time?" asked the other policeman.

"As you can see, gentlemen, he's still here," she said, slipping her arm through Jeffrey's. "But I couldn't have done it without you. Thanks again."

"Our pleasure, ma'am," the first one said. "See to

it that your friend gets you home before midnight or we'll run him in on . . . ah, heck, we'll think of something!"

She threw them a kiss as they drove away, and they blinked their lights and growled the siren before roaring back out onto the highway.

"Interesting entrance," Jeffrey said stiffly.

"I'm glad you approve," she replied.

She looked up at him and smiled beguilingly. Oh, boy, she thought. The man was about to have a fit! She figured there were several reasons for it. He'd been worried about her being so late. He thought she might have wanted to run him over when she'd pulled into the spot next to his car. He was angry with her.

When her smile didn't melt the polar ice in his eyes, she decided there was one more possible reason that he was upset with her: He was jealous because two police officers were so friendly with her. Whichever reason it was, she wasn't going to let it ruin the evening.

"Been waiting long?" she asked, smoothing her finger along the sleeve of his black evening suit.

"About half an hour," he said impatiently.

Ann was so beautiful, she took his breath away, he thought. But he wouldn't allow himself to be distracted by her beauty. Not yet.

"Care to share the humor of that little chase scene?" he asked.

"It *was* rather funny, wasn't it, how *I* was the one who appeared to be chasing a cop for a change?"

"It was a scream," he said icily. Then his reserve

broke. "Dammit, Ann," he yelled, making her jump. "Are you going to tell me what the hell's been going on or not?"

"Of course I am, Jeffrey," she murmured, lowering her lashes to conceal the humor in her eyes.

He apologized for yelling at her, then helped her into his car. "Just tell me, Ann," he said as he slipped behind the wheel. "When I saw you coming, I didn't know what to think."

"I'll tell you in as few words as possible." She slid across the front seat until her thigh was touching his. "Two miles down the road the cops stopped me for speeding. After they checked my registration and realized I was the owner of my car, we started talking about the Corvette Rallies that are held every three months outside town. They jointly own a Classic, too, you see."

She smiled and shrugged philosophically. "Well, before I realized it, several minutes had passed. I'd already been running late when I left River Regency, which is why I was speeding. I didn't get the ticket, by the way. Anyhow, when I explained where I was going and why, they offered to lead the way. End of story." She smiled brightly. "See, that didn't take long, did it?"

"Hell, no, it didn't take long. It sounds like you left out half the story."

Feigning nervousness, Ann fussed with the silk petals at her throat. "Oh, does it?" she asked softly.

"Annie, you'd better start explaining, unless you want me to get arrested for mayhem," he threatened, sliding an arm around her silk-clad shoulders.

"I told them that I had to get here before seven-thirty, or you'd leave me . . ."

"Let me see your tongue again."

"I didn't lie. I make it a point never to wait more than half an hour for anyone, and I figured a busy man like you might possibly have the same rule."

"I can't believe a couple of cops let themselves be conned into leading a two-car chase," Jeffrey said. But when he gazed into Ann's smoky blue eyes, and stared at her tulip-red lips and mysterious smile, he had to change his opinion. What man in his right mind could refuse her . . . anything?

Ann watched him moisten his lips as he gazed at her. She'd bet he wasn't thinking about cop cars anymore. She wanted him to kiss her. Right now. But she didn't want to dismiss the present discussion before everything was fully explained.

"Jeffrey?"

"Mmmm?" He blew gently at a wispy curl at her temple. It begged for his touch, and he complied. "What is it, love?"

"There's a tiny bit more to this story. I'd like to get it out of the way so we can forget it and enjoy our evening together."

"Sure, Annie. I'm all ears," he said, watching the curl wind around his finger.

"I'll be driving in the next Classic Rally," she said. "It's four weeks from Sunday."

"And the cops couldn't arrest a Classic driver, right?"

"Right! Can we go now? I'm hungry."

"In a minute, love." He trailed his fingers over her

cheek to her ear, then along her jawline to her bright red mouth. He leaned closer as he tenderly traced her parted lips. "I have to kiss you first."

She sighed with happiness, and he pressed his mouth against hers. Her heart leaped. She slid her hands up over his chest, taking note of his thundering heartbeat, then encircled his neck to draw his head closer. When his embrace tightened and he lifted her against his body, all her senses rejoiced. After a long, long separation, she felt as if she'd come home.

The Jade Room, one of the area's finest restaurants, was all Ann had expected and more.

"I've never eaten here before," she said after the hostess, dressed in a gold and green kimono, escorted them to their table. "How did you know about it?"

"The man who drove for me last week suggested it," Jeffrey said. "I think he knew what he was talking about."

The intimate room was completely dark except for the individual lights that shone down from the ceiling directly onto each white-cloth table. A single flame-red hibiscus in a slender ebony vase graced each table. The effect was dramatic, yet romantic too.

"This is very lovely," Ann said. "I'm glad I'm here with you."

"I'm glad you're here too," he said. "I've never dined with a more exquisitely beautiful woman." Gazing directly into her eyes, he lifted her hand to his lips. He kissed her palm, branding it with molten heat. "I'm falling under your spell, lovely lady. I may never be able to escape."

Ann closed her eyes, savoring the moment while his fervent kiss sang through her veins. When she opened her eyes again, she smiled. She brought his hand to her cheek and rubbed against it in feline pleasure. She brushed her lips across his knuckles, the tip of her tongue burning a moist trail. Jeffrey sucked in his breath, and she felt his long fingers twitch in an involuntary spasm.

His eyes seemed to burn into hers. "I may never *want* to escape," he corrected himself.

She released his hand and rested hers in her lap. "Stay with me only if you want to stay."

"Annie love. I definitely want to stay with you. Can we be together tonight?"

She hesitated for only an instant. "Yes, darling, I want that too."

The instant Ann said the words, she felt lightheaded, as if she'd drunk too much champagne. Tonight she would become Jeffrey's lover. Regardless of who he was, what he was doing here at the River Regency, she would give herself to him joyously, with no reservations. She gazed across the table at him, adoring the strong planes of his face, the hair brushing across his forehead, his beautiful blue eyes, his sensual lips—which were moving.

Ann pulled herself from her dreamy reverie. "I'm sorry. What did you say?"

He laughed. "I like it that I can have that kind of

effect on you, Annie. I asked if you knew what you wanted to eat."

Embarrassed at being caught staring, she opened her menu and muttered, "No." Later, after they had been served their food, she drew in a deep breath for courage. Come on, she told herself. Let's get it over with so you can put this spying aside forever. "How was your day?" she asked.

"Long," Jeffrey said, winking roguishly. "I played golf all afternoon. Can you see how my nose got sunburned?"

She leaned forward. His nose was as gorgeously tanned as the rest of him. "Sorry you got burned," she said, patting his cheek.

He coughed over his chuckle. She had no idea how much he'd gotten "burned" today.

"Was this a business meeting?" she asked.

"No. Today was just a friendly game."

He had to smile at his less than accurate explanation. He'd played with Charles today, the man who'd taught him the rudiments of the game. When one played golf with Charles, it was strictly business. You played . . . and then you paid!

"Gosh, it must be nice," Ann said teasingly, not really interested in finding out the name of his partner. "Sleep all morning. Golf all afternoon. When do you work?"

"I had to wait for some people today," he said. "Sometimes decisions take longer than I'd like, but there's not a thing I can do about it."

He smiled and shrugged, but she didn't return his

smile. Was she concerned about his career? he wondered.

"I assure you, Ann, I have a very successful business. Seven people work for me. They do a lot of the legwork."

"Are you a good boss?" she asked.

"The best." When she didn't respond, he raised an inquiring brow. "Don't you believe me?"

"I'd want to hear what your employees had to say first," she said, sidestepping the issue. Then she drew in a long, steadying breath and smiled at Jeffrey. "I want to leave now," she said, placing her napkin beside her plate. "That is, if you're ready."

Jeffrey sighed with relief. Somehow he'd had the distinct impression she was going to change her mind. But no, everything was all right. He'd been mistaken. Tonight would be theirs to hold forever in their hearts. It would be their beginning.

"I think I've been waiting for you all my life. Just for you, love," he whispered, placing a lingering kiss on the inside of her wrist. "I'm more than ready, Annie. Let's go."

Six

Jeffrey thought they'd never get back to the hotel, what with driving to the mall to get Ann's car, then following her back to the parking garage. Sneaking around was not his style. He disliked not being able to be completely honest with Ann, particularly when that insistent inner voice kept telling him this relationship could last a lifetime. If he was lucky.

He didn't want to do anything that might jeopardize Ann's trust in him, particularly tonight. But it wouldn't be much longer. As soon as he got the evidence against his mother's guilty employee, he could tell Ann the whole story. He knew she'd understand why he had to operate undercover.

As Ann drove she wondered how, when the time came, she'd explain to Jeffrey's satisfaction why she'd spied on him, and for whom. He was an entrepreneur, someone who answered only to himself. Would he understand how important it was for her to remain loyal to the River Regency corporation? Loyalty had always been a virtue she valued. As was honesty, she thought, feeling decidedly guilty.

At the hotel they met in the shadows of the side terrace. The night breeze caressed their faces, and the throbbing notes of a vintage love song flowed through the open French doors.

"Dance with me, Ann," Jeffrey whispered, drawing her into the haven of his arms. "I want to hold you."

He was an excellent dancer. One hand pressed firmly against her back, just above her waist, easing her ever closer, fitting her torso against him so that his leg slid between her thighs with each step. His chin rested at her temple, and his warm breath feathered the wispy curls on her forehead. Her hand lay curled inside his, resting on his chest.

He lowered his hand to the small of her back, arching her pliant form as he performed a hesitation step, then whirled her in a tight circle. Wanting, needing to mold her body along the full length of his, he lifted her right hand to his shoulder and began to massage her back with both hands.

At first his touch was a gentle, gliding caress. Twirling her again, he could feel her breasts press against his chest. His exploring fingers became bold, thoroughly examining her from shoulders to hips. Suddenly his breath hissed out from between his teeth.

"Do my hands deceive me, Annie?"

"I seriously doubt it," she said, laughing softly.

"Lady, you are absolutely full of surprises," he said gruffly. "I'm glad I didn't discover you weren't wearing anything under this dress while we were dining." He dropped his hands to her rounded bottom and pressed her against his burgeoning manhood. "I probably would have made a damn fool out of myself!" he said, groaning. "Kiss me!"

She lifted her face to his. His tongue searched her mouth with insistent strokes. Satin heat, rough velvet, moist sweetness. Her fingers played through his leonine mane, and her body surged against his. Jeffrey's arousal was so intense, it was almost painful as he caressed her, the heels of his hands kneading the soft rounded sides of her breasts. When the sweet torture ended, both of them were breathing raggedly.

"My room number is 217," she whispered.

"It's etched in my mind," he said, turning away from her to gaze at the stars.

"I'll see you there?"

He gulped back a chuckle. "You bet."

"Will you be long?"

Good Lord! he thought, valiantly holding back his laughter. "I'll be there as soon as I'm able, Annie. Believe me, I don't want to stay here a moment longer than I have to."

"Oh!" she exclaimed softly. "I'm so sorry."

"Darling, never be sorry for what your body does to mine," he said, his backward glance practically singeing her dress. "Will you please get going . . . before I drag you into the bushes?"

• • •

By the time Jeffrey arrived at Ann's room, she had opened the doors to the balcony and found some romantic music on the stereo. The room was softly illuminated by one lamp on a bedside table and a fat candle on another table in front of the small sofa. She opened the door for Jeffrey and leaned against the frame, smiling up into his sexy blue eyes. He grinned, winked, and handed her a bottle of an expensive champagne.

"If you don't have glasses, we can take a bath in it," he said hopefully.

"I have glasses," she assured him.

He whistled with surprise as he followed her into the room, beautifully decorated in delft blue and ivory. "How does a trainee rate a place like this?" he asked. "You must have had one heck of an agent negotiate your contract." What was going on? he wondered. He'd just realized the hotel didn't provide employee accommodations. It was against house rules. Ann wasn't a trainee?

Think! Ann ordered her whirling brain as she walked to the wet bar for glasses. Why hadn't she suggested going somewhere else? Like *his* room. Well, it was too late now. She'd just have to talk her way out again.

"Don't start playing detective," she warned him, setting the glasses down on the table. "I pay rent."

He raised a brow skeptically.

"A subsidized rate, I'm sure," she added hurriedly. "I was told management keeps this room for emergency quarters. And I was certainly in the middle of an emergency. You see, my belongings got lost in transit. I have an apartment leased in town, but until the moving company finds my furniture, I'd be sleeping on the floor."

Did he look like he was buying her story? she wondered as he poured the champagne. She just wasn't certain. "I sure was lucky no one else was using it."

"It was nice of the hotel to arrange it," he agreed, though he was still sure something was not quite right here. But when he handed Ann her champagne and looked into her eyes, his interest in why she was living in this room fled.

Ann smiled at him as she took the glass, hoping he would drop the subject about her living quarters. They clinked their glasses together and drank the bubbly wine, their gazes locked. Then Jeffrey took her glass and set it down on the table with his.

"No more talking," he said.

He sat on the sofa and tugged her down onto his lap. She went willingly. After all, he was doing exactly what she wanted him to do—forgetting everything else and beginning to make love to her. He kissed her deeply, and almost instantly she forgot too. His kisses had a drugging effect on her.

Mindlessly she loosened his tie and slipped it slowly from around his neck.

"Yes, sweetheart," he whispered. "I want to feel your hands on me."

She unfastened the first two buttons on his fine cotton shirt, then leaned forward and kissed the warm flesh she'd revealed. Her fingers continued quickly unbuttoning his shirt, uncovering more and more of his bronzed chest.

"That's it, Annie," he said. "Touch me." He took his jacket off and pulled his shirt from his pants. "Your hands set me on fire."

Excitement swirled through Ann as she smoothed the crisp golden curls on his chest, twirling, designing, then smoothing them in another direction. Her lips followed suit, stringing moist kisses across his warm flesh. When her tongue flicked across one flat brown nipple, he gasped, and one hand cupped the back of her neck, holding her to him.

"Annie," he whispered, and lifted her head. He branded her mouth with a kiss so intoxicating and exciting, she dug her nails into his back, hanging on so she wouldn't explode like a Roman candle. When the kiss ended, they both were breathing heavily. Jeffrey stood up, holding her in his arms. "I need more room, Annie. I want to love you in comfort."

She nodded, then buried her face into the side of his neck, inhaling his cologne and his own heady aroma. She did not speak while he carried her toward the bed. He stopped near the opened door to the balcony.

"Nice view," he whispered, sliding her down along his body until her feet touched the floor.

"The stars are pretty tonight," she agreed, slowly pushing his shirt from his broad shoulders. "And it's warm too.'"

"It's going to get warmer, love."

"Shall I bet on it?" she teased softly.

"You'd be betting a sure thing." He removed the

pins from her smooth chignon, and his breath caught when her hair cascaded like a shimmering waterfall into his hands. "Oh, Annie," he murmured. "You are so very beautiful."

"I was thinking the same thing about you," she said, trailing her hands lightly over his hard chest.

"Men are not beautiful."

"Just proves how special you are."

"I want to see how special *you* are."

She met his blazing blue eyes, standing straight and tall. He brought both her hands to his lips, kissing each fingertip and her palms, then lowered her hands to rest at his waist. His own hands then stroked up her slender silk-clad arms to her shoulders.

They smiled at each other when, in the distance, they heard the call of an owl along the wooded banks of the river. Then Ann lost contact with the world as Jeffrey kissed her explosively and slid the zipper of her dress down her back.

Air swirled across her exposed skin, and she would have shivered if Jeffrey hadn't drawn her into his arms, molding her against his warm body. His fingers grazed along the length of her spine, then he slipped the dress from her shoulders.

She whimpered with dissatisfaction when he broke the kiss. He pulled back slightly, and his tender gaze drifted across her exposed shoulders, creamy white against the ebony silk. Then his eyes met hers, and he could see how disoriented she'd become.

"He's calling his mate," he whispered.

"Who?" she asked dazedly.

He smiled. "That's right, love." Slowly he eased

her dress down her body to the floor. "Oh, Annie," he breathed. "You're a goddess."

Though her bathing suit had concealed little two days before, he still wasn't prepared for her magnificent beauty. Her long dark hair cascaded down her straight back. The black velvet ribbon at her throat was enchanting, and its white flower gave her features an ethereal quality.

But when he let his gaze burn over the rest of her—her firm breasts and soft belly, her flaring hips and trim thighs, which cradled the dark nest of her femininity—he knew Ann was all woman, and very much real.

He pulled her to him and ran his hands over her black silk stockings. Then slowly he stripped them from her, kneeling to slip her high-heeled shoes off. He stood, and she watched his eyes darken as he gazed at her. Again he slid his hands up her arms to her throat, then lowered them to her breasts. He lifted each creamy globe, molding, fondling, rubbing his thumbs across the hardening peaks.

"You are exquisite," he said, and leaned down to kiss one nipple. He lavished attention on it until it was a dark rose and pebbly-hard, then turned to the other, drawing it deep into his hot mouth.

Ann arched against him as she felt a throbbing sensation in her womb. Her fingers threaded through his hair, massaged his neck, trailed over his shoulders. She felt the strength drain from her legs and clung to him.

"Jeff, I can't stand."

"I've got you, love." He swept her into his arms

and carried her to the bed, then gently laid her on the cool satin spread.

Ann almost fainted with the force of a new thought. Perhaps Jeffrey *did* have her. Perhaps she had already fallen in love with him.

"Can you take this off, Annie?" he asked, toying with the flower beneath her ear. "We can't be sure if it's poisonous."

"But it's not real, Jeff," she said, her gaze drawn hypnotically to the golden hair arrowing into his trousers.

He chuckled softly, tipping her head so she'd look at his face. "I was teasing, though I do want you to take it off. I don't want anything between your lovely soft neck and my lips."

Looking at Jeffrey's handsome face didn't help Ann's concentration much. He had the sexiest, bluest eyes she'd ever seen. Without looking away from him, she unfastened the little hooks under the flower and handed the velvet choker to him. He placed it on the nightstand, then stood to strip off his clothes.

"I've been waiting for you," she said as he lay down beside her, his naked body hard and hot against hers. "A long time."

"Sweetheart," he murmured, gathering her in his strong arms. He dipped his head to nuzzle her neck, nibbling gently. When she sighed and arched her head back, giving him greater access, he chuckled. "You have such a succulent throat, Annie." He comically bared his teeth and widened his eyes. "Makes me feel like royalty just to be near you."

"Listen, Count. If you do, I will too," she warned, laughing.

"You're no longer under my spell," he said sadly, trailing kisses down into the fragrant valley between her breasts. "Oh, well, I'll just have to find something else to do." He drew one nipple deep into his mouth and inhaled deeply. "Mmm. You smell wonderful."

"Thank you," she said primly, then giggled and patted him on his head.

She knew the teasing was over when he captured her mouth with his and kissed her passionately, without reserve, sending her little-girl giggles right out the window. Her arms encircled his neck, bringing him ever closer to her. His hands smoothed over her, gliding across silken belly to silken thighs, then back to silken curls. She writhed beneath his touch, her body opening to him, fluttering, pulsating.

"I feel like I'm falling," she whispered, clinging to his shoulders.

"Shhh, baby," he murmured. "Just let it happen."

"But . . ."

"We're falling together . . . in love. Remember?"

She sighed, then kissed him. "I remember, darling. Please. Please, Jeff, come to me."

He held her close. "Be patient a little while longer, my love," he said. "I promise, it will be worth it."

"I want you," she pleaded. "I need you."

But Jeffrey resisted the temptation. He wanted to make their first joining one Ann would always remember. He already knew he'd never forget.

He watched her carefully as he stroked her, and

smiled with satisfaction when she caught her breath. She began rocking her hips, and he increased the intensity of his caresses, coaxing a response. Finally she cried out, surrendering, her body arching off the bed in ecstasy. Desire shot through him as he felt the throbbing pressure around his fingers, but still he waited. When the pulsating beat subsided and she collapsed back onto the bed, he lifted his body over hers.

Sighing contentedly, she embraced him. "That was lovely," she said breathlessly, and kissed him.

"I'm coming to you now, Annie."

She smiled and smoothed a golden lock of hair back from his blazing blue eyes. "But I'm all worn out."

"You'll catch a second wind," he promised, and kissed her until she begged to be let up for air. Then he slid inside her, savoring how her soft, hot tightness gloved his length.

"How does that feel?" he asked.

"Mmmm, marvelous." She stroked his back languidly. "But I'm still too tired to move."

"Wanna bet?"

He pulled back, then thrust into her with such surging force, her eyes opened wide and she gasped with surprise. She was so filled with him, she felt she might burst . . . but in a most compelling, vital way. Then she could no longer think as her greedy body began to match his rhythm, lifting and arching to meet his strong thrusts as he carried her higher and higher into the stars.

"That's it, love," he whispered, his arms tightening around her. He squeezed his eyes shut, struggling to maintain control for a while longer. "That's it. Move with me."

"It's . . . it's . . ." She cried out. "Jeff . . . it's happening again!"

She clung to him as her body seemed to explode into thousands of brightly colored pieces. Jeffrey felt her tighten around him, and let himself go. Together they burst into the heavens, wrapped securely in each other's arms.

"I'm flying!" she cried in awe.

"I'm with you, Annie!"

Afterward they lay exhausted, sprawled across the cool, slippery spread as they slowly fluttered back down to earth.

"I can't believe it," Ann said.

"I wanted you to be completely satisfied, sweetheart."

"But that wonderful feeling. And twice!"

"It never happened before?"

"I don't kiss and tell," she murmured sleepily. It was difficult to find the strength simply to form words, much less whole sentences. "What would you think of me?"

"Hey, Annie, you're among friends here."

"Well . . ."

"Come on, Annie, tell me. Has it ever happened to you before?"

She drew in a deep breath, then exhaled on a sigh. "Only in my dreams."

Smiling tenderly, he kissed her lips, then her closed

eyelids. "I'm very glad it happened for the first time with me, honey."

"You are."

"I just said I was."

"No, no," she mumbled. "I wasn't asking a question. I was making a statement. *You are.*"

"I are what?"

"Special."

"So are you, love."

Seven

Jeffrey awoke in his own bed. He glanced at his watch and discovered it was very late in the morning. Smiling, he stretched and rolled to his feet. What a night! he thought, recalling every moment, the way Ann had felt in his arms, beneath his body. Each little cry, each little sigh. He couldn't remember another time when he'd been so happy.

"Ah, Annie, you're truly amazing," he whispered, stretching again. He had no idea where she got so much energy, though he'd bet she was feeling stiff and sore this morning. They'd made love most of the night. As soon as he showered and shaved he'd call her, he decided, strolling into the bathroom.

Downstairs in the accounting office, Ann covered a yawn, then squirmed to a more comfortable position on the hard desk chair. Her job today was to provide secretarial services for any of the hotel's guests requiring them.

But, oh, she thought, last night had surely been a night to remember. In one evening's time she'd become knowledgeable, experienced. Had learned how to please and be pleased. She had had no idea lovemaking could be so wonderful.

She'd try to call Jeffrey later, she decided. She'd been so sleepy when he left at dawn, she'd forgotten to tell him where he could find her today.

She yawned again, then rose from her chair. She had to move around a little or she was going to fall asleep at her desk. The trouble was, she felt awfully stiff. Into how many positions had her body been molded? she wondered. Each one had given different sensations to different parts of her anatomy. All had left her satiated, yet eager to learn more.

Unannounced, that little nagging doubt in the back of her mind came trundling to the forefront, making itself heard. What was she going to do if Jeffrey Madison turned out to be an executive raider? Maybe she ought to think about it now.

Could she love him and remain a loyal assistant to Vanessa? If she couldn't do both, then she'd have to leave this fine hotel and find another position . . . in Utah. But only if Jeffrey knew that she loved him, and returned that love. Otherwise, what would it matter if she loved him? Corporate raider or not, she'd stay right here. If he did not ask her to share his life, what would anything matter?

Meanwhile Jeffrey had finished his shower and was taking care of business at Mountainview. After he hung up the phone he thumped his pillow in disgust. What in the world was happening? he wondered. No counterbid from a rival hotel for his fake convention had arrived at his office. Had the U.S. Post Office gone on vacation? Or had he misjudged all three of the River Regency executives?

"Dammit," he muttered. One of them had to be the tipster. He had that old gut feeling about it. But he knew it wouldn't do any good to worry. It would all come together on time, he told himself, paraphrasing one of his dad's old sayings. Absently he ran his hand across his bedspread, and suddenly the picture of Ann's body wrapped around his, lying on pale blue satin, filled his mind.

She was so very special. So beautiful. So sincere. So loving.

Loving? his heart repeated. As in love? He pondered the word for a long time. Of course he was in love, he realized finally. Ann Waverly was the most wonderful woman he'd ever known, bright and gorgeous and fun. How could he not love her? And why else had he called her "love" almost from the first day they'd met? He'd never used any endearment even approaching that four-letter dilly before. The word had always been anathema to him.

He drew in a long shuddering breath, then grinned drunkenly. "I love Annie," he whispered. "I *love* her."

Suddenly he wanted to shout it from the rooftop. He wanted to spell it across the sky, carve it in stone in perpetuity. He wanted everyone in the world to know what had happened to him. He was in love with the most lovable, loving woman in the world.

What would happen if he asked her to share his life? he wondered. Would she leave the hotel business to come live at Mountainview? Could he expect her to sacrifice her career just for him?

It was all so confusing, he thought, raking his fingers through his hair. How could he ask her to make such an unfair compromise? Actually it wouldn't be a compromise at all. It would be a trade-off.

"My love for her career," he said aloud. "Oh, hell!"

Whistling off-key, he dialed her room number. He continued whistling while the phong rang, then finally admitted she was not going to answer.

Where was she? he wondered. Someone else had brought his coffee and morning paper. Someone else had knocked on the door a few minutes ago to clean his room. His compulsion to find her was overwhelming, so he dressed quickly and took the elevator to the lobby. He searched for her at the registration office, the concierge desk, even the luggage room, all in vain.

Where the devil could she be? he fumed, standing by the lobby fountain, his legs spread wide, his arms akimbo. Then he grinned and snapped his fingers. "Call Mom," he said softly. He'd insist she find out where her unknown trainee was stationed today. It would give her something to mull over, he thought, chuckling as he hurried back to his room.

"I don't know what you expect of me, Jeffrey," his mother said after he'd called her and made his request. "Have you forgotten? Not only am I your mother, I am the owner of this establishment. I don't know where it's written that I shall also be your social secretary. Why do you want to know where this Ann Waverly is anyway? She can't go out with you. It's house—"

"Rules," he finished. "I know, Mom. Would you just indulge your only son? Please?"

She did, but under strict protest. "She's the standby stenographer today. But I don't want you to bother that girl, Jeffrey. Do you hear me? The day manager tells me she's an excellent employee. Perhaps I'd better meet her for myself one of these days."

"Maybe you will . . . one of these days. Thanks, Legs. I love you."

"Hey, Waverly," her boss for the day called to Ann. "Can you take dictation straight to the 'writer? There's a guy on the phone who needs a confidential secretary."

"Sure, Marty, I can do it. What's the room number?"

"Eleven-oh-eight. A Mr. Madison."

"Hi, Annie," Jeffrey said when he opened his door. "Come on in." Was any woman more beautiful, more kissable, more dear? he asked silently.

"You requested a secretary? That's me," she said, smiling, fully expecting to be swept off her feet and into his arms. Was any man more handsome, more little-boyishly lovable? she mused. But why was he acting so shy? Was he embarrassed about last night? Had she been too forward? Well, she certainly wasn't going to take the first step today.

"I really need a secretary, Ann," he said, not meeting her eyes. "Honest!"

"That's why I'm here, Jeffrey. It's my job." Hurriedly she set up her typewriter and plugged it into the wall socket. "Ready whenever you are."

To her surprise he dictated nine letters before he took a breather.

"Here are both the originals and the carbons, Jeffrey," she said, slipping the sheets into a manila folder and handing it to him.

He thanked her and carried the folder over to one of the cabinets in a large wooden unit on the far wall. He unlocked the cabinet and set the folder inside. Before he closed and relocked the door, Ann saw something that shocked and dismayed her. She was unable to keep the look of horror from her face, and Jeffrey saw it when he turned back to her.

"I have to deal with some unusual people at times," he said. "I have a permit to carry it."

"But a gun! Oh, Jeffrey."

What was he going to do with a gun? she thought frantically. Handguns hurt and killed people. They were designed to do that. What business was Jeffrey really in? Perhaps she'd been wrong all along. Perhaps he did something a lot worse than steal executives. She had to get away from him and make her report to Vanessa.

"If you're finished with your dictation," she said. "I'll leave now." She had a difficult time keeping her voice from quavering, and was not successful in controlling her trembling hands as she gathered her things.

He stopped her. "I'm going to need you a while longer," he said, not meeting her questioning gaze. He walked over to the phone and called the accounting office.

"Hello," he said. "This is Mr. Madison in 1108." He paused. "Yes, everything's fine. I wanted to tell you that I need Ms. Waverly for at least two more hours. Is that a problem? No? Good. Will you have two carafes of coffee sent up at once then? Thank you."

He began dictating letters again, pacing more and more agitatedly across the wide sitting room. What in the world was wrong with him? she wondered. No personal conversation, no kiss. Hardly a smile. And now she'd found out that he owned a handgun.

If he cared at all for her, why was he acting this way? *And you believed him when he told you he was falling in love with you,* said her heart, refusing to beat for an instant. His pacing increased until Ann wanted to scream and run from the room. Fortunately, just at the moment when she thought she couldn't stand it anymore, room service arrived with their coffee.

"Let's take a break, okay?" Jeffrey asked.

"If you wish," she replied. "Would you like me to pour?"

Cups in hand, they both gravitated to the large picture window overlooking the concrete pond and artificial garden.

"I sure hate that plastic landscaping," Jeffrey said.

"I'm not crazy about it either," she agreed. "I like natural surroundings."

He turned to her. "Like your meadow?"

She met his eyes and nodded. As he gazed at her Jeffrey tried to figure out what she was feeling. What she really wanted. Damn, this was ridiculous, he thought in disgust. They were acting like teenagers. He should just get on with it.

"Do you like it here?" he asked.

"Very much," she said. "I told you that before."

What was he after? she wondered distractedly. He was acting like a hunter, stalking her.

"Ever consider taking another job?" he went on. "Something with more money?"

Was he trying to recruit her? Surely, he wouldn't want to hire her away from the River Regency. He thought she was only an entry-level trainee.

He took a deep breath. "I could promise you work with much better conditions than you have here."

There was no mistaking his motives now, she thought. Her heart constricted with pain. He wanted her to work for him. Or . . . She looked away in humiliation. Good Lord, did he want her to be his mistress? It was more than she could stand.

"I can't work for you, Jeff," she said, her heart sinking.

"Great!" he shouted.

Ann almost jumped out of her skin, she was so surprised by his exuberant exclamation. She looked at him, and was thrown completely off balance when she saw his seductive smile. Then the adrenaline began to flow, and outrage overcame her reticence to speak.

"What the hell do you mean, great?" she yelled, facing him, her clenched hands on her hips. "You're not playing with a full deck if you think I'm going to work for you. Didn't you hear me? I said no. And if you think I'm going to change my mind, you're taking a sucker bet." When he did not reply, but began to move in her direction, she started all over again. "Jeffrey Madison, I am not going—"

"That's why I'm glad," he interrupted, slipping his arms around her waist and drawing her close to his body. "I'm glad you refused, because I was really hoping I could interest you in something more personal. Come here, sweetheart," he whispered into her ear. "I need to love you."

"Now, wait just one darn minute," she said, breaking free and backing away from him. "If you think I'll quit my job and come to your damn mountaintop as your mistress, you're crazier than I thought you were."

He chuckled softly as he stalked her, finally backing her into the wall. "How about coming to my mountain as my wife?"

Ann was glad she had something to lean against. "Your wife?" she said, swallowing hard. "You're asking me . . . Is this why you've been acting so strange today? I thought you were angry about something when you kept pacing the room."

He smiled sheepishly. "I was trying to work up my courage, honey."

She searched his eyes as if she could find the answer to this puzzling conversation there.

"I love you, Annie," he murmured, gathering her in his arms. "I want you to be my wife."

"Oh, Jeffrey," she whispered. "I love you too."

Could any words sound so sweet? she wondered as he carried her to the huge four-poster. He loved her. He wanted her to be his wife.

He set her down in the middle of the bed, then began removing her clothes. He slipped off her jacket and kissed her throat while he unbuttoned her blouse. After sweeping the blouse from her shoulders, he trailed kisses down her back. He unfastened her skirt, and she lifted her hips so he could slide it off her. Then he whipped her slip up over her head, laughing when she almost fell over because of his haste.

"Oh, Annie, you are so precious to me," he said, catching her in his arms. "I haven't any patience left, love, so please bear with me while I bare you."

She groaned at his pun, but allowed him to hurriedly strip away her lacy bra and sheer panty hose and panties. When he sat back on his heels and gazed admiringly at her body, not moving, she began to squirm.

"Now that that's finished," she said, "what do you propose we do next?"

"My haste in undressing you is only an example of my impatience, love." His smoldering gaze swept over her ivory skin. "Now I want to make love to you." Smiling, he reached for her.

She was too quick for him. She pushed him back onto the bed and knelt above him. Smiling wickedly, she leaned down and kissed him. When she was through, his breathing was harsh and labored.

"Now, love?" he asked.

"Uh-uh." She freed her hair from its topknot and spread the silky dark strands like a tent around his head. "I demand equal rights."

He laughed. "I believed in equal treatment under the law, long before it became popular."

"A good thing too." She unbuttoned his shirt and pushed it off his shoulders. "You must have had a liberated mother." She leaned forward and nipped his neck, then trailed her hot tongue to his nipples.

"My mother," he said between gasps, "tried to teach me to be an understanding man." He shuddered when she rubbed her breasts against him.

"It's a shame she let you get so spoiled," Ann murmured as she unbuckled his belt and slid down his zipper.

"I am not spoiled, Annie."

She scampered off the mattress and pulled him to his feet. Standing on tiptoe, she kissed his chin. "Well, I suppose you did inherit that prominent chin," she said as she slipped her hands inside his jeans and briefs. Before he could say anything, she skimmed them down his legs.

"Annie, stop this," he ordered. "I feel like I'm going to be strip-searched."

"You are also very, very bossy, Jeffrey Madison." She knelt at his feet. "Take off your shoes so you can step out of your pants."

"Talk about bossy!" he shot back, but he did her bidding. "I don't know how any man could enjoy making love with a bossy bro—"

He froze in mid-sentence as her hands slid back up his legs and closed around his aching manhood.

"Oh, Annie! Oh, love, you do have a way of moving right to the heart of the matter." He moaned as she continued to caress him, then allowed her to push him back onto the bed.

"Shall we see what I can remember from last

night?" she asked. She began to explore his hard body with feather-light touches and incendiary kisses. "I'll bet you'd like this," she murmured. "And this. And how about this?" She grinned mischievously when he trembled and clutched her shoulders. "Have I got you covered?"

"I'm fading," he said hoarsely. "I don't think I have a chance in this game. I'm folding."

"Not quite yet, darling," she said. She straddled his hips and began the serious business of making love to the man she loved.

Yes, she loved him. There wasn't a doubt in her mind now. And he had asked her to be his wife. Shocked by the realization, she sat up straight and cried out.

"Darling, what is it?" Jeffrey was instantly alert, stroking her face, taking her hands in his strong grip. "Did you hurt yourself, sweetheart?"

"You did suggest that we should get married, didn't you?" she asked, leaning down until her nose almost touched his.

He smiled lovingly. "Yes, sweetheart, I did." He lifted his head to kiss her.

"You do mean to each other, don't you?"

He chuckled at the expression on her face. "That's exactly what I had in mind."

"But we don't have that much in common," she cried, sitting up again.

He moved against her suggestively. "Oh, I don't know about that," he said as he released her hands to massage her hips.

Ann's body had received his unspoken message,

even if her brain had not. She dropped her chin to her chest and moaned softly. "But my job. Your job. Different ways of living."

"But we share the same way of loving," he said, inhaling deeply. "Uh . . . Annie love? I know you think this is a very important conversation, but do you suppose we could postpone it till later?" He smoothed his hands along her sides to caress her firm breasts. "I don't think my mind's on talking right now." When she smiled seductively, he knew she agreed.

"We're going to make love now, darling," she whispered. She began to move over him, threading her fingers through the thick golden hair on his magnificent chest.

His hips rose beneath hers, matching her movements, driving home the throbbing shaft of his manhood.

"Just lie back and enjoy it," she murmured. "I'll do all the work."

If Jeffrey hadn't been so caught up in their intimate ride to paradise, he would have laughed out loud. He couldn't have lain still if his life depended on it!

Eight

When Ann returned to her room, it was very late in the afternoon. After experiencing two hours of the most satisfying and fulfilling lovemaking, she should have been walking a foot above the ground, floating in the clouds, euphoric. Instead, she felt dismal, her emotions in a turmoil.

With tears in her eyes, she twisted her long hair back into a topknot, fastening it with a wooden skewer, and stepped into the shower. She always thought best in the shower, and she had a great deal to think about.

The hot, hard spray of water pounded against her neck and spine and the backs of her legs. As she inhaled the steam, her thinking cleared. She loved Jeffrey Madison. For better or worse, she loved him.

But who was Jeffrey Madison? Was he an executive recruiter as he said? Or were his intentions even more ignoble than those of a headhunter?

She thought about the gun locked in the heavy wooden cabinet in his room. Just the mere idea of his owning and carrying a gun—permit or no—made her shiver. Why did a man carry a gun? To protect himself and others in his care. Or to force others to do his bidding.

But what did he want others to do? she wondered, frantically searching her mind for some clue. Not three hours ago Jeffrey had offered her a new position as his wife. But at first she hadn't known that was what he'd meant. She smiled at the ludicrous picture that popped into her brain: Jeffrey, dressed like an outlaw from the Old West, whipping his gun from his low-slung holster and drawing on her. Well, she thought, he had . . . in a manner of speaking!

Ann gave her head a firm shake. Fantasizing about Jeffrey's advanced course in lovemaking was not going to solve her problem. She could feel her heart crack under the strain of decision. She loved Jeffrey. She was loyal to Vanessa and the River Regency. Tears of despair filled her eyes, and she felt them slip down her cheeks.

When she had shed all her tears, she stepped out of the shower, wrapped herself in a thick terry robe, and walked stoically to the phone. She knew what she had to do. So she did it.

"Mrs. Cummings?" she said when Vanessa answered her phone. "This is Ann. I have to see you at once."

Vanessa agreed, and Ann had no sooner hung up

the phone than it rang. She jumped in alarm, as if it were a bomb that threatened to go off in her hand.

"Hello?" she said.

"Hi, Annie," murmured a deep, familiar voice. "Were you sleeping, love?"

"Not yet. I just took a shower."

"Me, too," he whispered. "I wish we'd been to-gether. We could have experimented again."

"I think we did rather enough experimenting as it was, don't you?"

"Your voice sounds all husky and sexy. Do you suppose you'll always sound like that after we make love in the afternoon?"

No, Jeffrey, she thought sadly. *I always sound like this after I cry.* "I'm just tired," she said. "I need to rest before this evening."

"Rest, darling," he whispered. "I'll see you at seven-thirty. Dream of me, love."

Half an hour later Ann was pacing the length of her boss's inner office. She felt Vanessa's gaze follow her back and forth across the thick carpet.

"Ann," Vanessa said, "please tell me what's wrong."

Ann turned to face her boss, her teeth clenched against more tears. "I've just returned from Mr. Mad-ison's suite. He made a proposition . . . and he has a gun."

"Jeffrey Madison Cum—came here with a gun? My Lord, he held you prisoner with a gun? I'll have him arrested at once." She hurried to the phone.

"No, no, Mrs. Cummings," Ann said, rushing across

the room to stop her. "Not that kind of a proposition. He offered me a different position. Somewhere else, and . . ."

"A different position?" Vanessa asked. "What kind of a position?"

"It doesn't matter, Mrs. Cummings. Right now I'm not completely convinced he was serious."

"But he did offer you a job this afternoon while . . ." She glanced out the window. "Would you mind telling me what you were doing in this—this criminal's room?"

"He needed a typist, and that was my job, for today. When he locked up his papers, I saw a gun. He says he has a permit."

"A likely story."

"I believe him. I can't think of any reason why he would lie," Ann insisted.

"Well, I can think of about ten," Vanessa said, and ticked them off on her fingers. "He could be planning a heist in St. Charles. Even here at the River Regency. He could be a hit man." She gave Ann a steely stare and hit her palm with her fist. "Why, that man could be planning to waste someone right in our very own lobby!"

Ann could not suppress her grin. If nothing else, this visit with her boss was giving her a laugh. "Where in the world did you learn to talk like that?" she asked. "You sound like a gun moll."

Vanessa laughed and fluffed her ash-blond hair. "I read a lot. And my son . . . my somnambulism keeps me awake at night."

Ann looked at her suspiciously. "How can you be kept awake by sleepwalking?"

"Well, dear, it's like this," Vanessa said, sitting down at her desk and fussing with some papers. "If I . . . ah, didn't read for hours at night, that's what I'd be doing. Yes, that's it. I'd be walking around in my sleep." She clucked her tongue and fanned her suddenly flushed cheeks. "Terrible habit, that. Now, where were we?"

"Trying to figure out what to do with Jeffrey Madison."

"Ah, yes. I think we should confront him with all this evidence, then throw him out on his ear."

"How can we do that?" Ann asked. "The evidence is all circumstantial."

"I'll think of something."

"He's smart enough to hit you with a lawsuit if you aren't on sure ground."

"I can at least have him arrested for suspicion."

"Of what? Jeffrey hasn't done anything but offer me a job."

"And are you interested in taking it?"

"I thought I was a few hours ago, but now I'm not entirely sure."

Vanessa reached for the phone again. "Then I'll have him evicted for harassing one of my employees."

Ann beat her to the receiver. Placing her hand over it, she gazed at her boss. "Do you have to do anything at all? Can't we just hope he leaves? I can even ask him to leave. Wouldn't that be a better plan? No bad press or anything."

Vanessa tipped her head to one side and looked

consideringly at Ann. Her lips were pursed, her right brow arched. "Ann? Have you fallen in love with this man? This—this hooligan?"

"He's not a hooligan," Ann said, raising her voice. "He's a fine, wonderful, kind man. He's—" Then she realized to whom she was talking. "I apologize for yelling, Mrs. Cummings. Please forgive me."

Vanessa continued to study her. "I will repeat my question, Ann. Do you love Jeffrey Madison?"

"I . . . I . . ."

"Well?"

"Yes, *yes*! Heaven help me, but it's true." To her embarrassment, she began to cry. "I don't know what I'm going to do," she wailed, suddenly finding herself wrapped in Vanessa's maternal embrace.

"There, there, child. It's all right. Everything will straighten itself out. Don't cry."

"But *how* can everything straighten itself out?" Ann asked. "I don't know where to turn."

Vanessa wiped the tears from Ann's face, then gave her a string of orders. "First, young lady, you are to go to your room, lie down, and put a cool cloth on your forehead. Next, you are going to take a long nap. Sleep will do you a world of good. Last, you're going to trust in luck."

"Luck?" Ann repeated scoffingly. "The Lady has not been very friendly lately."

"As one of my dear friends who's succeeded the hard way says: Luck is nothing but preparation meeting opportunity."

"Then I suppose I wasn't prepared to fall in love,"

Ann said, sniffling. "How else do you think I got messed up with a felon?"

"Ann Waverly, who are you calling a felon?"

"Jeffrey Madison. Who else?"

"Now, dear, we don't know that for a fact, do we?"

"No, but . . . aren't you starting to change your tune?"

"Only because I've considered your good advice about bad press, et cetera," Vanessa said. She fluttered her hands at Ann. "Go on now. Shoo! Get some rest. I'll talk to you in the morning."

Back in her room Ann climbed naked into bed and laid a cool damp cloth over her burning eyes. Every muscle in her body ached. It was not an entirely unpleasant feeling because she knew *why* her body hurt. But the ache in her heart was almost more than she could bear.

Should any of this change her decision—Jeffrey's supposed profession, the gun in his room—now that he'd professed his love? she wondered. Asked her to marry him? Said he wanted to share the rest of his life with her?

Being honest with herself, she knew her first impulse would be to grab him and run like hell. But it took only a moment to realize what a big mistake that would be. Yes, she wanted to share her life with Jeffrey. She loved him. But how long would her love for him endure when she knew it was built upon a false premise?

She tried another tack. Suppose none of the things

she suspected turned out to be true? her logical mind asked. Then what would you do? She squirmed under the covers, pressing the cloth against her eyes as she again felt the sting of tears. If Jeffrey were really an honest, ethical man who'd asked her to marry him and go with him to Mountainview to live happily every after, she'd know exactly what to do. She'd leave everything behind to take the biggest chance of her life. It would be worth the risk.

But she couldn't gamble with her heart until she knew the odds she was playing. And she didn't know.

"Oh, dear Lord," she said softly, and rolled over to curl into a ball. Until she knew the truth, she and Jeffrey couldn't even discuss the kind of compromises they'd have to make, about where they'd live and how and for how long. She couldn't accept his proposal under these conditions. Like it or not, she knew she needed her career together with a marriage. She'd discovered that about herself long ago. She truly did not think she could change.

"But I love him," she cried. She pounded the bed, railing at her frustration. "And he loves me," she whispered. "With all my heart, I know he loves me." She sighed tremulously. "Damn, damn, damn!"

Heartsick, she decided she couldn't see him again until she knew the truth. If, as she suspected, he were trying to lure key employees away from the River Regency, that would destroy any relationship they'd had. Even if he were pure as the driven snow, what kind of a life could they have together anyway?

Wonderful, exciting, rewarding, shouted her heart.

Tears spilled down her cheeks again. "It would never work."

Ann woke with a start. She thought she must be very sick because she heard a ringing in her ears. She shook her head and sat up, then finally realized the ringing was the phone. She groaned and fell back onto her pillows, reaching for the receiver.

Her hand froze in midair.

She couldn't answer her phone. Ten to one it would be Jeffrey. She squinted at her clock. It was after eight o'clock. He'd be calling to find out why she hadn't met him for their date. How would she be able to explain her reasons? No, she decided, it was far better just to let the phone ring. She could leave a message for him at the desk so he wouldn't come pounding on her door later.

When the incessant ringing stopped, she sighed in relief. But in moments it began again.

"Stop ringing, dammit," she screamed at the phone. "I won't answer, so just stop."

At the other end of the line Jeffrey slammed the receiver down, then shoved open the door of the phone booth and jogged to his car. He paused and searched the mall parking lot and the stretch of highway one last time. Nowhere could he see a little red car. Ann's little red car.

"Where the hell is she?" he grumbled.

In the next instant he condemned his impatience. Suppose she'd had an accident? he thought, his stomach twisting with sudden fear. Quickly he slid behind the wheel of his car and started the engine, then pulled out of the parking lot with more speed than good sense.

The trip back to the hotel seemed interminable. He forced himself to drive at a slower speed than he would ordinarily, glancing into the ditches on either side of the road. Whenever he passed a service station he slowed to a crawl until he was sure there was no red automobile there.

When he pulled into the hotel parking garage and found Ann's car sitting in its usual spot, he still did not consider that she'd stood him up. He worried that she was ill. In the lobby he walked over to the registration desk and asked if there were any messages for him. The clerk handed him an envelope. He opened it at once.

"Exhausted. Forgive me," the note read.

"What the hell?" he muttered.

"Something wrong, sir?" the clerk asked.

"What?" He glanced up from the cryptic message. "No, nothing."

He walked over to the garden lounge and hoisted himself up onto a high stool at the bar. After ordering a double vodka on the rocks, he reread the typed message.

When his drink arrived, he took a long swallow, then another, before he tried to decipher the hidden message contained in those three words. After two more long swigs of his drink, he started to relax and a smug grin tugged at the corners of his mouth.

"Dearest, darling Jeffrey," he rewrote in his head. "This afternoon's lovemaking was beyond belief. Your kisses, your caresses, your . . . *everything* left me weak. I don't know where I found the strength to return to my room. I should have stayed with you. I wish I had.

"But now that I am here, in my own room, in my own bed, and all alone, I am filled with vivid memories of you. I try to move, but I am exhausted. It is a most satisfying lethargy, I can assure you."

He envisioned her in her bed, leaning back against the pillows, her hair spread around her as she gazed lovingly into his eyes. He sighed, straightening his shoulders, then finished his drink and ordered another.

Well, he thought, that took care of the first word. Now on to the second and third, "Forgive me."

He closed his eyes and imagined a sleepy, satisfied smile on her sensuous lips.

"Forgive me," she would say. "I want so much to share the night with you, my darling. I want to dine with you, dance with you, feel your hard body pressed against me. I want to greet the dawn in your arms. In your bed. Beneath you. With you inside me. But, dearest Jeffrey, you have drained me. I must rest now. I want to be with you. You know that. Forgive me until tomorrow, my darling. Then I'll make it up to you. I promise."

He sipped his drink, grinning for no reason in particular. It was amazing, he decided, how much information Ann had been able to pack into those three little words.

• • •

At seven o'clock Thursday morning Ann called Mike, the manager of the parking garage. She was supposed to work for him that day, but she told him she was sick and wouldn't be able to make it. After she hung up she lay back in bed, hugging one of her pillows to her chest. She buried her face in its cool softness. If she inhaled deeply, she could still identify Jeffrey's cologne. This only proved to Ann that she did indeed need a day off, away from work, from the world, from Jeffrey. She was sick, as sick as could be. But no doctor could help her, because she was sick at heart.

Two hours later Jeffrey had swum his customary fifty laps, showered, shaved, and eaten an enormous breakfast. Those two—or had it been three?—double vodkas last night had calmed him nicely, he thought. He'd slept like a baby.

Reading Ann's letter of apology had helped too. He didn't even consider that all those words, except three, were his.

Now it was time to find out where Ann was working today. He had had no idea there were so many jobs involved in running a large hotel. There hadn't seemed to be so many different positions when his folks had owned Mountainview Inn. Of course, that had been a much smaller operation, and not as luxurious. It was still operated by a single family— the Angelinos—but he'd heard they were putting it back on the market next month because they were moving to Europe. He wondered how much they wanted for it. A germ of an idea began tickling at the back of his mind.

He stood near the elevators in the lobby, considering where he should begin his search for his Annie love. He could always call his mother and ask her. But she was probably curious enough already. It was a wonder she hadn't sent out the troops to spy on her only son just because he'd mentioned Ann's name a couple of times.

No, he'd tough it out all by himself. After all, he was supposed to be a pretty sharp detective, wasn't he? Always got his man, right? His heart was quick to ask him if that also applied to "his woman"? Strolling to the registration desk, he grinned broadly because he knew the answer. Annie loved him, had said she wanted to be his wife. True, they had a lot of discussion and compromises ahead of them, but with Annie at his side, all things were possible.

"Hello, Mr. Chapman," he said to the registration clerk, reading the name on the pocket of the man's uniform. "I wonder if you could help me. I'm trying to locate my cousin. She works here. Her name is Ann Waverly. Do you know where I might find her?"

Mr. Chapman was most helpful. Within a minute he was able to direct Jeffrey to the parking garage.

"Ask for Mike, sir. He'll be able to help you."

Jeffrey smiled and thanked the man. It took him ten minutes to find Mike. After he'd been informed that Ann Waverly had taken a sick day, it took Jeffrey exactly sixty seconds to make it back to the lobby and a house phone.

Ann answered the phone on the fourth ring. "Hello?"

"Did I wake you, love?'

"Yes, you did."

"The garage manager told me you were ill. What's wrong, Annie? Do you need a doctor?"

Pulling herself to a sitting position, Ann wiped her eyes with the back of her hand and finally came to her senses. She was sitting here, talking in her sleep, to *Jeffrey*!

"I don't want to talk to you," she said.

He chuckled. "Annie, I can't catch any germs through the phone."

"That's not what I mean. I really don't want to talk to you. Good-bye."

"Wait! Why are you acting like this? What's wrong?"

"You can't do what you're doing to my employer. It's unethical."

"Annie, what the hell are you talking about?"

She drew in a long breath, then sighed mournfully. "Oh, Jeff! If you don't know, then I can't help you. Good-bye."

When she hung up she was sure she could feel her heart breaking. Jeffrey stared at the phone. Finally accepting the fact that she'd hung up on him, he slammed the receiver into its cradle.

"Women!" he said in disgust. "Who the hell needs them?"

What in the world was wrong with her? And what the hell was she talking about? It was obvious Ann didn't know that her employer was his mother.

"You can't do what you're doing to my employer," he said in a mocking, falsetto voice. "It's unethical."

Operating on automatic pilot, he trudged to his

car and left the hotel. He didn't have any specific destination in mind, but wasn't surprised when he realized he was heading in the direction of Ann's meadow. He wondered if he could find it.

He had no trouble recognizing the gravel road off the highway. But then it took him almost an hour to find the hidden entrance to the meadow. He drove past it three times before he finally got out of the car and walked the half mile of road where he felt certain it was. After he found it and drove onto the rugged trail, he was careful to shut the gate. He'd given his word to keep Ann's secret. Even if she never talked to him again, he would keep her meadow secret.

If she never talked to him again? he repeated silently. "Oh, Annie love, please forget you ever said that," he whispered. He rubbed his eyes against a sudden glare that had made them water. At least that was what he told himself.

When he reached the meadow, he remained in his car for a long time, thinking, remembering. After what seemed like an eternity, he dragged himself from the seat and slammed the door closed. Leaning against the front fender, he let his gaze wander over the peaceful land.

There was the spot where they'd spread the blanket and had their lunch. The grass had not quite recovered. His heart beat more rapidly, his breathing grew ragged as he recalled more of that afternoon.

What a beautiful body Annie has! he thought, smiling. Long and voluptuous and satin-smooth. And her wild cloud of silky hair. He grinned as he remembered that postage-stamp-size swimming suit she'd worn. He hadn't been certain at first it would stay on. And when they had kissed, and he'd felt her warm body beneath his for the first time, it was heaven. He was getting aroused just from the memory. If it hadn't been for Ann's ragged-around-the-edges iron control . . . Grinning and shaking his head, he climbed back into his car.

At the Mosey Inn he ordered a hearty soup and spinach salad for lunch. He sat at the same table where he and Ann had dined that first night. Afterward he strolled outside to the porch. He couldn't bring himself to sit on the cushioned glider, though. He didn't want to be here alone. He didn't want to be here at all, he thought, and left the inn.

Driving back to the hotel, he recalled how they'd talked of their life-styles and where they liked to live. Ann had said she needed the excitement of the hotel business. She loved it. He had said he couldn't breathe in the city. But if they were sensible and discussed it, he was sure they could find a compromise. "*If* she ever talks to me again," he muttered. Unheralded, a picture of the Mountainview Inn appeared in his mind.

He drove past the golf course and recalled their game. She was the first woman he'd played with who was as good as he.

He parked his car in the hotel garage and went back to his suite. He wanted to stop thinking about Ann, but knew he couldn't. He yanked on the drape cord and the curtains swept open. Gazing out the large picture window, he relived their first night together.

She had made her smashing entrance with the police car escort and thrown him for a loop. He had never seen a more beautiful, vivacious woman. He'd felt proud and tremendously lucky that he was the one to escort Ann to the Jade Room. And later, in her room, he'd been thrilled by her free spirit, her caring, loving ways. He had wanted so much to please her, and believed he had. There wasn't a man alive, he was sure, who did not dream of outrageous, delightful, erotic play with a love goddess.

His pleasant reverie was rudely interrupted when his brain reminded him that he was forgetting one very important point. Ann did not wish to speak to him ever again.

He began to pace from room to room, a frown creasing his brow. "Dammit!" he muttered. "She can't do this to us."

Without allowing himself to dwell upon his decision, he strode to the phone and dialed Ann's room.

"Hello?"

"Ann, it's Jeff. Now, don't hang up on me. *Please.*"

How could he do this to her? Ann wondered. She should hang up. She needed to think. But her traitor voice kept talking to the man she loved.

"What do you want, Jeff?"

Oh, Annie, he thought. If only he were with her this instant, he'd tell her exactly what he wanted. He'd show her. "We need to talk, love."

She sighed. "I need to think. . . ."

"Let me come to your room."

"*Alone.*"

"Two heads are better than one," he said, trying to tease a little laugh from her.

"Not in this case. I get all confused when I'm with you. Then I can't think at all."

"Is that a fact? I had no idea I could do that."

"You can take it to the bank," she assured him on a sigh.

"You do the same to me."

"I find that difficult to believe." He was trying to take advantage of her vulnerability, she told herself.

"We could open a joint account, Annie," he said huskily, hoping his words would sizzle right into her heart and help her to break free of the barriers she'd put up against him. "Let me come to you, love."

"Not now."

"When? Tonight?"

"No, perhaps tomorrow," she answered, trying to put him off as long as possible. She had to weigh what she knew about him, what she thought she knew, and what she suspected was true. It was so darned confusing, only more so, because she loved him.

"Do I have to wait that long, honey?"

"Yes, you do. I have a great deal to think about. Now, please don't call me again."

"Think fast, Annie," he said. "Tomorrow is D-day."

"What do you mean?"

"Decision day, honey. I love you." He waited patiently for a moment, then knew she wasn't going to respond. "Good night."

Nine

The break in the hotel case came at ten-thirty the following morning. Kim called Jeffrey to make her report.

"The letter came half an hour ago, Jeff. Special delivery."

"What name, Kim?" he asked eagerly. "Which company was it addressed to?"

"Caracas International. Isn't that the name you gave to—"

"Mark Ludlow, the general manager. He must be getting *some* cut of the profits if he'd inform against the River Regency. My mother pays him a first-rate salary plus bonuses."

"Either that, or he sells himself cheap," Kim said.

"Either way, he's a bastard. Thanks for your help."

"No problem. Go get 'em, boss."

Jeffrey immediately went to his mother's penthouse and told her. She sent for Ludlow. When the general manager saw Jeffrey, all color drained from his face.

"Is it necessary for us to parade all our proof before you?" Vanessa asked.

Ludlow hung his head and looked ashamed of himself. "That won't be necessary, Mrs. Cummings," he said, his voice breaking.

"Mr. Ludlow, you are hereby fired, effective immediately. Your final check is waiting for you in Accounting."

Jeffrey watched as the man seemed to age ten years in the blink of an eye. Why didn't people realize that there was no free lunch? he thought with disgust.

"You came with high recommendations, Mr. Ludlow," Vanessa said. "I hope you realize that I cannot provide you with the same."

Ludlow nodded.

"I will, however, release a memo to the staff explaining that you have resigned, effective immediately, to accept another position in another city."

"Thank you, Mrs. Cummings."

She turned away, wrapping her arms around her waist. Lifting her chin, she blinked rapidly as she stared out the window at the river below. "You are dismissed."

After Ludlow had gone, Jeffrey gathered his mother into a big bear hug. "Come on, Legs. You did the right thing."

"I know." She sniffled delicately. "But I never quite get used to doing it. Your father used to tell me

that I'd never be tough enough to fire someone without hurting almost as much as the ex-employee."

"Shows what a neat lady you are, Mom. You've got
heart."

"Thank you, darling." She patted his cheek and
gave him a bittersweet smile. "Now then, don't you
have someplace to go? I have a mountain of work to
do."

He leaned down and kissed her briefly on the lips.
"I'm out of here."

"You're out of this world, darling."

"Aw, Legs, I keep telling you. You're prejudiced."

It took Jeffrey almost forty-five minutes to find
Ann. She was still assigned to the parking garage.
As he jogged up the ramp to the third level, he
finally spotted her. She was seated behind the wheel
of an old Cadillac that looked about a block long.

"Hi, Annie," he called, strolling over to the car.
"I've been looking all over for you, honey."

She turned her head and sent a glare his way that
almost knocked him over with its intensity.

"What's wrong?" he asked, his stomach curling
into a knot.

"What's wrong?" she screamed. She threw the car
into gear and laid rubber for a hundred feet before
she careened the lumbering giant into a parking
spot. The screeching protest of the brakes could be
heard all over the garage.

Jeffrey stood where he was, not knowing if she
was going to get out of the car . . . or turn the damn

thing around and try to ram him into a concrete wall. Whatever was bothering her, she was about as mad as he'd ever seen anyone.

Then he saw a transformation that made his blood run cold.

She climbed out of the car, slammed the door, and methodically locked it, then turned and walked toward him with slow, measured steps.

"Annie love?" He actually felt like taking a step backward, but held his ground. "Annie, we have to talk."

"You did it, didn't you?" The words stuck in her throat but still sounded to her like a death knell. And they were. Tolling the moments until her love for Jeffrey would completely die.

"What are you talking about, Ann? Did what?"

"Convinced the general manager to accept your offer."

"Ann, you don't know what you're talking about."

"He's gone, Jeffrey. How much longer before you get the public relations director and the convention manager?"

"Let me explain."

"Headhunter! That's what you are. I told you I couldn't forgive you for that."

"You're coming with me." He grabbed her hand, almost crushing it in his hard grip.

"Stop this. I'm not going anywhere with you."

"Like hell you aren't, Ms. Waverly."

He dragged her behind him. At the exit of the garage Mike got up from behind his desk and stood at the door.

"Is there a problem?" he asked, glancing from one face to the other. "Anything I can do to help?"

"Yes, Mike," Ann gasped. "I'm being—"

"She's been called to the office," Jeffrey interrupted. "There's an emergency, Mike."

"Hope it's nothing serious," Mike said, stepping aside.

Inside the hotel lobby Jeffrey took Ann's elbow in an iron grip and marched her toward the elevators.

"I suggest you keep walking, Ms. Waverly," he said when he felt her trying to lag behind, actually skidding on her heels to slow him up. "And I wouldn't advise you to make a scene in the middle of the lobby either. It would be a very tacky thing to do at the River Regency."

Ann looked around anxiously, trying to catch one of the other employees' attention. She sighed in relief when she saw Charles get off the penthouse elevator.

"Charles, help me," she said frantically. "Stop this lunatic. Call the police. Do something."

Charles halted in front of the pair, a puzzled expression on his dark face. "Jeffrey, where are you taking this sweet little girl?"

Jeffrey stood toe to toe with his good friend. His grip on Ann's arm did not decrease. "Out of my way, Charles. Ann and I have a few things to get straightened out."

When the man wisely moved aside, Ann was jerked past him into the elevator. She watched Jeffrey pull a key from his pocket and insert it into the elevator lock. The doors glided closed and with a tiny whoosh the elevator began to rise.

"Where did you get that key?" she asked snidely. "Steal it?"

Jeffrey would not permit himself to give her even a cutting glance. His anger was beginning to reach the boiling point. In another second or two, Mt. St. Helens wouldn't have a thing on him.

"Well?" Ann prodded. "Did you steal it, Jeffrey? Are you also a thief?" Her own anger was burning off some of the pain in the place where her heart had once dwelled. He'd stolen that too.

"Be quiet, woman."

She jerked her arm away and backed into a corner. "I will not be quiet. Where do you think you're taking me?"

"To see your boss."

The doors opened at that moment, and Jeffrey grabbed Ann's hand again. He pulled her off the elevator and into his mother's office.

Vanessa was seated at her desk, inspecting some papers. When Jeffrey and Ann burst into the room, she lifted her head and looked from one angry red face to the other. Then she met her son's fiery eyes, and smiled pleasantly.

"Yes, what is it?"

"I've had about all I can take for one day," he said, "so I brought Ann to you. Will you please tell this addle-brained woman why the hell I'm here?"

"Of course I will, Jeffrey." She turned to Ann. "Jeffrey is an investigator of white-collar crime. He's been working on a case for me. I'm going to share a confidence with you now. Mr. Ludlow did not resign for a better position. I fired him."

"But why?" Ann asked, completely bewildered.

"He was helping our competition underbid us on convention business. He was one of three suspects. Jeffrey helped me get the proof I needed to take action."

Ann's rosy cheeks became wan. Now that she knew the complete story, so many other parts of the puzzle dropped into place. Jeffrey was not an executive recruiter. He had been working undercover for Vanessa. Then why had Vanessa let her think . . .

"But you let me think he was a headhunter," she said. "Why didn't you trust me? I can't believe that you didn't."

Her outrage galvanized Jeffrey to his mother's defense. "Why should she trust you, Annie? This was a major business problem. You're being trained for a lower-level position. Surely, you don't think you're equipped to handle executive decisions."

That did it! Ann snatched her arm away from his grasp and marched to Vanessa's desk. She planted her feet firmly in place and balled her fists on her hips. And almost broke the glass in the picture window with her narrowed, incensed glare.

"I've about had it with this guy," she said angrily. "Will you tell this obnoxious bully who the hell I am?"

Smiling, Vanessa obliged. "Certainly, my dear." She turned back to her son. "Jeffrey, Ann is training to be my personal executive assistant." She savored the expression on his face. She'd wager his chin dropped at least four inches. "You did say I should ease up, didn't you, dear?"

Dumbfounded, all Jeffrey could do was sputter for several seconds. Then he found his voice again and stepped forward. "But why the unorthodox job switches?"

Vanessa continued to smile as she rose from her chair and walked around to the front of her rosewood desk. She reached up to pat Jeffrey's cheek. "Haven't I always done things my way, darling?"

The two continued to stare at each other, and Ann stared at both of them, sensing that she was waiting for another shoe to drop. Jeffrey looked as if he were going to have a stroke. Such a red face! Then he expelled a gust of air.

"Mother!" he said.

Mother?

"Now, son."

Son?

Ten

Ann almost fainted when she heard Jeffrey and Vanessa speak. Mother? Son? What in the world was going on here? In a daze she staggered over to the sofa and collapsed on the soft cushions.

Her mind simply refused to accept this piece of information, much less digest it. She began to rock back and forth, staring out the window, but seeing nothing.

Vanessa was the first to speak. "Jeffrey Madison Cummings, look what you've done to this poor girl."

Waving his arms, Jeffrey began to pace back and forth across the room. "*I've* done?" he yelled. "My own mother does a double-cross and then blames me." He turned and shook his finger at his mother. "Legs, I warned you about that crazy intrigue stuff."

Ann moaned, bringing Jeffrey's attention back to her. Moaning himself, he rushed to her. He fell on his knees before her and took both her hands in his, patting them. "Ann," he said frantically. "Look at me. Talk to me." When Ann only shook her head, he turned to his mother. "Help me, Mother," he pleaded.

Vanessa smiled at her son. "You seem to be in an ideal position to do something constructive, darling," she said as she walked toward the door. "I have to go downstairs now to schedule some interviews." She blew Jeffrey a kiss. "I love you, son." And then she was gone.

Jeffrey was too upset to notice how calm his mother had appeared all through this ordeal. Beside himself with worry, all he could think about was Ann. His Annie.

He stroked her pale cheeks with trembling fingers. Crooning her name, he tried to look into her eyes, hoping to make her focus on him. But she continued to stare blankly out the window.

"Annie love. Darling," he said. "Speak to me, sweetheart. *I love you.* I've loved you almost from the first night I got here." Tenderly he kissed her cheek, smoothing his lips to her temple. "Listen to me, Annie. I . . . love . . . you."

Ann blinked. Once, twice, then she turned her head to look into his clear blue eyes. Oh, she thought dreamily. Jeffrey had the most beautiful eyes in all the world. In them she could see how much he loved her. It was there for everyone to see. But especially for her.

"I love you too, Jeff," she replied, sighing tremulously. Tears began to fall, spilling unheeded down her smooth skin. "I thought I'd never be able to tell you again."

They fell into each other's arms, both trying to kiss away the pain. Jeffrey brushed her hair away from her damp face; Ann traced his mouth, now curved in a jubilant smile.

"Oh, love," he said. "I don't ever want to be separated from you again." He kissed her. "I thought I'd die when you refused to see me."

She laughed. "I've spent happier hours myself. But I thought you were stealing people from my boss."

Suddenly she stared at him. "Jeffrey, *my* boss is *your* mother!"

"How can such a beautiful woman be so intelligent as well?" he asked in a teasing tone before he kissed her breathless.

Distracted by unfinished business, Ann gently pulled from his embrace. "Jeff . . . your mother. She knew. She knew exactly what was going on. She planned it." Ann shook her head. "Why would she do all this? And to us?"

Jeffrey's face lit up with a big happy grin. "I guess she couldn't pass up a sure thing," he said, carefully wiping a tear from the corner of Ann's eye. She had the most beautiful eyes in the world, he thought fondly.

Ann still did not quite feel herself. Too much had happened. Her mind was not as sharp as usual.

"What sure thing?" she asked, blinking again.

"My mother loves it when a plan comes together."

"What plan?" Good night! she fumed inwardly.

She knew she hadn't always been this dense. What in the world was wrong with her?

"You'd better hang on tight, Annie. I think you're going to be in for another shock."

"Jeffrey, don't beat around the bush. After what I've found out so far today, nothing else could shock me."

"Don't bet on it, love."

She let him hold her hands in his strong clasp. Not because she was nervous, she assured herself. It just felt very nice. Furthermore, she thought Jeffrey was really making too much of this . . . whatever it was.

"Jeffrey, I think you're just sensationalizing a very small piece of information."

"Well, you're half right, I suppose," he admitted. "These things would start out very small."

She could feel life coming back into her limbs, her body, her heart, her brain. It was time to finish this debate.

"Jeffrey, I'll lay you ten to one odds that your information will not shock me," she said. "Now, tell me. What's this plan all about?"

"Grandchildren."

If Ann had been chewing gum, she would have swallowed it. "Wha—?" she gasped, unable to cover her surprise . . . and shock! Then she laughed. Now she knew where Jeffrey got his chutzpah. "You win, Jeffrey Madison."

"Cummings."

"Oh, yes," she agreed. "That too."

He brought her hands to his lips and kissed each

palm as he continued to gaze deeply into her smoky blue eyes.

"Marry me, darling."

The smile slipped from her lips. "Oh, Jeffrey, I want to marry you. I want to be your wife. But it wouldn't work. You love Utah and my place is here at the Regency. Or somewhere in the hotel business." She blinked as crystal tears again began to flow. "It's my profession, Jeffrey. You've got to understand."

"I do understand, love," he murmured, kissing her tears away. "We can work it out. Don't cry. We'll find a compromise," he promised. "We'll find it together."

"But what?" she asked.

"I've been toying with an idea," he said. "The Mountainview Inn is for sale. I happen to know the owners." He chuckled. "Heck, I know the original owners."

"You do?"

"My folks built it almost forty years ago. I was raised there and know every neat hiding place, from the attic to the wine cellar."

"But . . . then you know the hotel business."

"And I hate it."

"Oh!"

"But then, I don't have to run it." He stroked her cheek, then kissed her tenderly. "That would be your job."

"I'd be mistress of the inn?" She was fascinated by the idea.

"If that's what you want. Shall we bid on it, Annie love?"

"How much money would it take?" she asked, suddenly afraid.

"Sweetheart, don't worry about the money. I'll take care of the finances if you'll take care of the operations." He smiled, then winked. "Well, what do you say?"

"I say yes!" She leaned forward, her eyes sparkling with happiness, and gave him a kiss to seal their bargain. "Can we leave now?" she asked.

"For Mountainview? Don't you want to get married first? Shouldn't I meet your parents?"

Gently, she covered Jeffrey's mouth with her hand. "No, darling," she said throatily. "I was thinking of someplace nearby with some privacy."

"My room?"

"An excellent suggestion, Mr. Madi—oops, I mean, Mr. Cummings," she said, laughing happily.

He rose and brought Ann to his side, then crooked his arm for her hand. "Shall we, my future wife?"

"By all means, my future husband."

It was a good thing Jeffrey's suite was on the eleventh floor. They might have been half undressed in the elevator if it had taken any longer.

Seated on his large bed, Ann freed the top button of his shirt. "I think I'm going to love having my former boss for a mother-in-law." She released another button, then a third. "We think alike," she continued, smoothing the soft blue cotton shirt off his shoulders and down his arms. "I'm glad she didn't give up on you when you were a hotshot kid."

Sucking in his breath when Ann trailed her fingers over and around his nipples, Jeffrey tried to smile and retaliate in kind. "My mother can't have all the credit. Remember, my dad had quite a lot to do with my upbringing too." He tugged on the little pull tab on her uniform collar, and his eyes widened with pleasure when his handiwork revealed a lacy black camisole beneath her royal blue coveralls.

Ann's provocative sigh washed over him as he smoothed his hands inside, caressing her breasts, his fingers teasing and tantalizing the hardening buds. Soon her coveralls were stripped from her shoulders and lay in a puddle of blue around her hips.

Meanwhile Ann's hands continued their loving exploration as they wandered across his ribs and down toward his hips . . . and the zipper on his trousers.

"I'll bet," she murmured, "you've known Charles for a long time, too, haven't you?" She opened the snap with a vigorous yank.

"All my life," he whispered as she slid down the zipper. "Easy, baby. Be careful."

"He must have been in on this scheme too," she said, recalling her conversation with the man. "He didn't mention a word about knowing you when we spoke about you."

"He's a very loyal employee." Jeffrey slipped his hands underneath her black satin top and lifted it over her head. It fell to the floor, unheeded, and he reached for her long braid. He removed the fastener and methodically separated the three locks of black silk. Then he arranged the hair around her shoulders, smoothing it over her firm breasts with a decidedly sensuous intent. He smiled tenderly when he was able to elicit a frustrated little sigh from Ann.

"What do you want, love?" he murmured, rubbing his hands over her hair and breasts again and again. "Tell me what you need, darling."

"I want you to kiss me," she said in a soft voice.

"My pleasure, sweetheart."

He continued to caress her, exciting her unbearably. His lips feathered across her cheek, her temple, her fluttering eyelids, the tip of her nose, and finally settled on her mouth. He plucked at her nipples as his tongue plundered her mouth, slipping in and out of the sweet heat of her kiss.

"I love to kiss you, Annie."

She moaned again and drew back. "Kiss me here," she said.

With trembling hands she swept away the veil of silk. Then she cradled each creamy globe in a palm, offering herself to Jeffrey.

"I want you to kiss me . . . here."

Was ever a woman more beautiful, more trusting? he thought wonderingly. "I love you, Ann," he said, circling her waist with his arms and lowering his mouth to her breasts.

When he drew a sensitized tip deep into his mouth, using his tongue in marvelously innovative ways, she shuddered against him, leaning into his touch. His hands stroked up and down her spine as her fingers trailed through his thick sun-streaked hair.

"I love you, Jeff," she whispered.

His blazing gaze scorched over her body. "Lie down, my love. I want to pleasure you."

Gently he eased her back against the pillows. As she kicked off her deck shoes, he slid the coveralls and her black silk bikini panties off her legs.

"Oh, Annie," he murmured, his gaze softened by his love. "I'll treasure you forever."

He tried to kiss every inch of her body. He was well on his way to success when he felt her tug insistently on his trousers, pulling them lower and lower off his hips. Sighing, he rose from the bed and shed the rest of his clothes.

Although he had never considered himself an exhibitionist, Jeffrey had to admit that he got a real thrill out of watching Ann look at his body. Her smoky gaze was intense, and he could feel its effect upon his manhood. Her eyes were like mirrors, reflecting what she was thinking, what she was feeling, what she wanted next. The fire of her scorching gaze burned him, excited him beyond his wildest expectations. At this moment he thought it would be a sure bet that Ann's gaze could arouse a saint. Heck, she could fan the flame in a *statue* of a saint!

Jeffrey was neither saint nor statue, and could resist her no longer. He knelt beside her and gathered her into his arms. As he pressed a hot kiss on her parted lips, he eased his body next to her. Their legs entwined, their lips explored and tasted and savored. Tongues tasted silky skin; teeth nipped firm flesh.

Ann's slender fingers explored his broad back as his hands scorched across her middle, searing along the shadowed valleys to the secret depths of her being. His burning fingers ignited passion's core, and she cried out for him. Emotions sparked, then flamed, until the fervor of their shared love raged between them, making them one.

No tender lovemaking this. Locked in passionate desire, both sought release from the wild, consuming heat. On and on they traveled, he surging into her, she capturing and holding him. Then, in a crystal-clear instant, they reached that lover's paradise where there is no past, no future, only now.

Wrapped in a warm embrace, Ann and Jeffrey rested. Never had any two traveled so far in so short a time. They sighed, spent and satiated, then smiled happily at each other. Jeffrey leaned over the woman he loved and kissed her tenderly. "*Now* will you be my wife?"

Assured of their future together, Ann could not resist prolonging her answer. "Equal partners?"

"You can bet your bottom dollar on that, sweetheart." He kissed her again. "You can be boss of Mountainview Inn. I'll be boss of Mountainview Services. And never the twain shall meet."

"I'd be very disappointed if they didn't," she teased, nipping at his neck.

"I don't think we're talking about the same thing, honey." He felt the rise in his loins and pressed against Ann to share the information.

"Perhaps not," she agreed, laughing softly.

"Well?"

She fixed him with a measured gaze and pursed her lips. "You're sure now? Equal?"

"Forever," he promised, nudging insistently and twisting until she parted her legs and welcomed him. "Now then." He groaned softly when she moved under him in perfect cadence to his passionate song. "Answer me."

"Yes!"

Just before they left earth again for another trip around the moon, they sealed their agreement with a four-star kiss.

THE EDITOR'S CORNER

We have some wonderful news for you this month. Beginning with our October 1987 books, LOVESWEPT will be publishing *six* romances a month, not just four! We are very excited about this, and we hope all of you will be just as thrilled. Many of you have asked, requested, even pleaded with us over the years to publish more than four books a month, but we have always said that we wouldn't unless we were certain the quality of the books wouldn't suffer. We are confident now that, with all of the wonderful authors who write such fabulous books for us and all the new authors we are discovering, our future books will be just as much fun and just as heartwarming and beloved as those we've already published. And to let you know what you have to look forward to, I'll give you the titles and authors of the books we will be publishing in October 1987 (on sale in September).

#210 KISMET
by Helen Mittermeyer

#211 EVENINGS IN PARIS
by Kathleen Downes

#212 BANISH THE DRAGONS
by Margie McDonnell

#213 LEPRECHAUN
by Joan Elliott Pickart

#214 A KNIGHT TO REMEMBER
by Olivia and Ken Harper

#215 LOVING JENNY
by Billie Green

Before I go on to tell you about the delightful LOVESWEPTs in store for you next month, I want to remind you that Nora Roberts's romantic suspense novel, **HOT ICE,** is on sale right now. As I mentioned last month, it's dynamite, filled with intrigue, danger, exotic locations, and—of course!—features a fabulous hero and a fabulous heroine whom I know you will love. He's a professional thief; she's a reckless heiress looking for excitement. When he jumps into her Mercedes at a stoplight and a high-speed chase ensues, both Doug Lord and Whitney MacAllister get more than they bargained for! I'm sure you will love **HOT ICE,** so do get your copy now!

We start off our August LOVESWEPTs with Patt Bucheister,
(continued)

who has given us another tender and warm story in **TOUCH THE STARS,** LOVESWEPT #202. Diana Dragas can't stand reporters because they destroyed her father's career as a diplomat. This causes problems for the handsome and virile Michael Dare, who is captivated by the beautiful Diana— and is, alas, also a reporter. Still, Diana can't resist this gallant charmer and allows Michael to sweep her away. When she discovers he's misled her, she has to make the most important decision of her life. As always, Patt has created two wonderful people whom we can truly care about.

Peggy Webb's newest LOVESWEPT, **SUMMER JAZZ,** #203, is as hot and sultry as the title suggests. Mattie Houston comes home from Paris looking for sweet revenge on Hunter Chadwick, the impossibly handsome man who'd broken her heart years earlier. Both Mattie and Hunter are certain their love has died, but neither has forgotten that summer of sunshine and haunting jazz when they'd fallen shamelessly in love—and it takes only one touch for that love to be resurrected. But all the misunderstandings and pain of the past must be put to rest before they can be free to love again. This is a powerful, moving story that I'm sure you'll remember for a long time.

Joan Elliott Pickart has always been well loved for her humor, and **REFORMING FREDDY,** LOVESWEPT #204, has an opening that is as unique as it is funny. Tricia Todd never imagined that her physical fitness program—walking up the four flights of stairs to her office—could be so dangerous! Halfway up, she's confronted by a young thief, and she shocks herself as much as the teenager by whipping out her nephew's water pistol. She threatens to shoot Freddy, the young criminal, and gets more than her man—she gets two men. Lt. Spence Walker, rugged, handsome, and cynical, is certain that Tricia, a bright-eyed optimist, is all wrong for him. So why can't he keep away from her? And furthermore, what is she doing when she's mysteriously out of her office at odd hours during the day? Actually, Tricia is doing exactly what Spence told her not to do—reforming Freddy. You'll laugh out loud as Tricia tries to deal with both Freddy and

(continued)

Spence, teaching each—in very different ways—that they don't have to be afraid of love.

Next, Susan Richardson's **A SLOW SIMMER**, LOVE-SWEPT #205, pairs two unlikely people—gourmet cook Betsy Carmody and hunk-of-any-month quarterback Jesse Kincaid. Betsy and Jesse had known each other years earlier, when Betsy was married to another player on the San Francisco football team. That marriage was a disaster, and she wants to have nothing to do with the big, mischievous, and handsome Jesse . . . but he doesn't believe in taking no for an answer and just keeps coming back, weakening her resistance with his sexy smiles and heart-stopping kisses. This is a charming love story, and Jesse is a hero you'll cheer for, both on and off the field.

Do I need to remind you that the next three books of the Delaney Dynasty go on sale next month? If you haven't already asked your bookseller to reserve copies for you, be sure to do so now. The trilogy has the overall title **THE DELANEYS OF KILLAROO**, and the individual book titles are:

Adelaide, The Enchantress by Kay Hooper	*Matilda, The Adventuress* by Iris Johansen
	Sydney, The Temptress by Fayrene Preston

Enjoy!

Sincerely,

Carolyn Nichols

Carolyn Nichols
   Editor
LOVESWEPT
Bantam Books, Inc.
666 Fifth Avenue
New York, NY 10103

It's a little like being Loveswept

SHEER MADNESS

SHEER COLOR

SHEER PASSION

SHEER EXCITEMENT

SHEER INTRIGUE

SHEER ROMANCE

All it takes is a little imagination and more Pazazz.®

Coming this July from Clairol...Pazazz Sheer Color Wash
—8 inspiring sheer washes of color that last up to 4 shampoos.

Look for the Free Loveswept *THE DELANEYS OF KILLAROO* book sampler this July in participating stores carrying Pazazz Sheer Color Wash.